0

**Mills & Boon® Medical™ Romance
brings you the final instalment
in the Heart of a Rebel trilogy
from favourite author Alison Roberts!**

*There'd been four of them once upon a
time. But, after the loss of their best friend,
now there is just Max, Rick and Jet. These
rebel doctors have formed an unbreakable
brotherhood—a bond that would see them
put their lives on the line for each other...*

Now these bad boys are about to be tamed!
But it'll take a special kind of woman
to see past their tough exteriors
and find the heart of a rebel…

In April you met Max and Rick,
and now it's time to introduce
the last of the rebel doctors—Jet!

The Heart of a Rebel
*Legendary doctors
who aren't afraid to break the rules!*

Dear Reader

OK. Personal confession time, here :-)

I'm one of those women who find certain tough, leather-clad men who ride powerful motorbikes irresistibly sexy.

Can this image be improved on?

I thought so. What if these men are also fabulously good-looking, highly intelligent, and capable of putting their lives on the line for the people they love?

For each other.

For children.

For their women.

These are my 'bad boys'. Max, Rick and Jet. Bonded by a shared tragedy in the past, but not barred from a future filled with love.

Enjoy.

I certainly did :-)

With love

Alison

THE
TORTURED REBEL

BY
ALISON ROBERTS

First published in Great Britain 2011
by Mills & Boon, an imprint of Harlequin (UK) Limited.
Large Print edition 2012
Harlequin (UK) Limited, Eton House,
18-24 Paradise Road, Richmond, Surrey TW9 1SR

© Alison Roberts 2011

ISBN: 978 0 263 22432 0

Harlequin (UK) policy is to use papers that are
natural, renewable and recyclable products and made
from wood grown in sustainable forests. The logging
and manufacturing process conform to the legal
environmental regulations of the country of origin.

Printed and bound in Great Britain
by CPI Antony Rowe, Chippenham, Wiltshire

Alison Roberts lives in Christchurch, New Zealand. She began her working career as a primary school teacher, but now juggles available working hours between writing and active duty as an ambulance officer. Throwing in a large dose of parenting, housework, gardening and pet-minding keeps life busy, and teenage daughter Becky is responsible for an increasing number of days spent on equestrian pursuits. Finding time for everything can be a challenge, but the rewards make the effort more than worthwhile.

Recent titles by the same author:

THE UNSUNG HERO
THE HONOURABLE MAVERICK
ST PIRAN'S: THE BROODING HEART SURGEON†
THE MARRY-ME WISH*
WISHING FOR A MIRACLE*

*Part of the *Baby Gift* collection
†*St Piran's Hospital*

**These titles are also available in ebook format
from www.millsandboon.co.uk**

Why not check out *Wishing for a Miracle*
by Alison Roberts—
a Dear Author recommended read.

CHAPTER ONE

A FIGURE clad completely in black emerged from the passenger seat of the vehicle.

Tall. Solid. Reaching for what had to be a heavy pack from the back seat and hefting it effortlessly onto one shoulder.

And then he turned and Rebecca could see his face under spikes of hair as black as his uniform. She could see the uncompromising features of a man she hated enough for the shockwave to steal the breath from her lungs and make her heart thump hard enough to be a painful tattoo against her ribs.

'No *way*.'

'What?' A grey-haired man, whose uniform bore the insignia of the largest rescue helicopter service New Zealand had to offer, moved away from the small cluster of people in front of a huge map that covered an interior wall of this upstairs office. 'Did you say something, Bec?'

The words had seemed like an agonised, internal groan, but apparently she had spoken them aloud. Maybe they'd had even more carrying power than reaching the ears of her boss, Richard. That might explain why the man outside had turned his head so swiftly to look up. Why his gaze had flown so unerringly to her face.

She could feel the way he stilled as he recognised her. Did it require an effort to shift the weight of so much guilt?

She hoped so.

'Ah…' The voice was now right behind her shoulder.

'Yeah…' She was testing her voice. Checking to make sure that it did not betray her. 'The medic's arrived.'

'Bit more than a medic.' There was a note of awe in her boss's voice as he raised a hand to acknowledge the new arrival. 'James Munroe is the best the army has to offer. Emergency specialist. Been with the SAS on and off for the past six years and he can handle anything. Perfect choice for a mission like this. Stroke of luck they already had a jet coming up here that he could catch a ride on.'

The incredulous huff escaped from Rebecca's tight chest all by itself. A sharp punctuation mark. Rather like the way James Munroe slammed the door of the vehicle behind him, adding a flat-handed thump that dismissed the driver.

'Problem?' Richard's tone was dumbfounded.

You have no idea, she wanted to say. Wisely, she pressed her lips firmly together and kept her eyes fixed on the flashing beacons of the airport security vehicle as it sped off, flanked by bright runway lights that stretched into the distance.

Lights that had looked as festive as Christmas decorations only minutes ago as she'd watched and waited for this arrival with all the excitement of a child expecting a special gift.

Dismay could feel rather like anger, couldn't it?

This was…unthinkable, that was what it was. After so many years of earning the reputation of being as tough as they came, unflinching in the face of danger and ready to deal with any emergency in a heartbeat, Rebecca Harding had a horrible feeling she might have hit the wall.

So she said nothing as she tried to deal with it.

The perfect choice for the mission had vanished from sight now, which was helping. He'd be going into the small side door of the hangar. Climbing the stairs to this office—the operational hub of this rescue service. She could get a grip on whatever was making it so hard to breathe. Think, even. Deal with this overwhelmingly unpleasant sensation that had to be…fear? No. She didn't do fear.

Creases in her bright orange flight suit vanished as she straightened to her full height of five feet four inches. Never mind that at least one of those inches came from the heels of her steel-capped boots. Her fingers tightened around the strap of the helmet dangling from her hand.

'Not having second thoughts, are you?'

'Are you kidding?' Rebecca actually found a smile. 'I've been waiting for a mission like this for my whole life.'

She had. This was *it*. A night flight to a destination outside any normal flight zone that would
push fuel capabilities. A volcanic Pacific island
that had been rocked by an earthquake and could
erupt for real at any time. A group of frightened
conservationists that were trapped and injured
and in desperate need of evacuation.

Oh, yes. Even in a career that had had more
than its share of excitement, this mission promised to be a highlight.

'Hmm.' Richard didn't sound entirely convinced. He stared at his top pilot for a long second
and then a spark of comprehension dawned on his
face. 'Don't tell me you and this James Munroe
have some kind of history?'

History.

That was a good word for it. The past. An event
momentous enough to wipe out your world. Or
rather to blot out the sun so that life became so
bleak that merely surviving seemed an impossible challenge.

Oh, yes. She and Jet had history, all right.

But Rebecca shook her head. She had made a

choice a very long time ago not to let the past rob her of a future. It would be easy enough to find another pilot who would be more than willing to take on this mission. Finding another medic with the kind of skills this one had would be impossible. The past few hours had been tense enough as search and rescue commanders put this plan together. They were hardly likely to tolerate a hiccup that was purely personal. Not when lives were depending on its success.

So her past had come back to haunt her?

So what?

She had been chosen and she was up for the challenge.

The real question was whether the willingness to deal with the situation would be reciprocated, and she was about to find out because the door of the office opened and her past walked in.

I hate you.

I hope I never have to set eyes on you ever, ever again.

Words that had been spoken more than ten

years ago and yet they were as clear in his head right now as if they'd just been uttered.

What on earth was Matt's sister doing in this room full of the men who were in charge of organising this urgent rescue mission that he'd just been flown in from his army base down south to be a part of? And why was she wearing a flight suit? Had she given up nursing to become a paramedic? Not that he was going to allow her to occupy more than his peripheral vision or thoughts at the moment. His attention was on the most senior-looking person in the group. The one who was coming towards him with an extended hand.

'James. Great that you could get here so fast.'

'Jet,' he corrected, his smile taut. 'Haven't answered to James in longer than I care to remember.'

Longer than the ten years since he'd last breathed the same air as the woman still standing by the window. He didn't need to look at her directly to be aware of how her shape had changed. He could even sense more than the physical maturity those curves under the overalls advertised. A curious mix of femininity and determination emanated from that side of the room like a scent but it wasn't quite powerful enough to wipe out the image of the girl he remembered.

A distraught teenager who'd pummelled his chest with her fists when he'd tried to hold her. Who'd told him that it was *his* fault.

That she would hate him for ever.

And that had been fair enough. He'd hated himself back then. Complying with the request never to be seen again had been no hardship. It hadn't been simply the guilt. It had been the gut-wrenching similarity she had to her brother.

The same wildly curly hair. The same dark eyes and cheeky grin. Not that any hint of a smile, let alone anything more joyous, could be detected from her direction. And even a grazing glance had shown that her hair was very different. Cropped so short the curls had gone but, if anything, that accentuated her eyes and they had always been a mirror of her brother's, with that darkness softened by a touch of vulnerability that drew an urge to protect like the most powerful magnet.

He may not have shared Matt's blood the way Becca did but they'd been brothers to the bone and the last thing he'd expected right now was the soul-piercing awareness of how much he still missed his best mate.

He was barely listening to the introductions being made to the other men. Senior representatives from search and rescue, civil defence and the navy.

'I understood I was the only medic being sent,' he growled, flicking his gaze sideways.

'You are. The auxiliary fuel tanks needed to go the distance which means there's no room for any other personnel.' Richard had seen the direction of his glance. 'This is your pilot, Rebecca Harding. She's just waiting for the mechanics to finish fitting the auxiliary fuel tanks.'

Pilot?

'What's the flight time expected to be?'

'Approximately four hours. Have you been briefed properly?'

'I'd appreciate an update.'

He was directed towards the wall map. 'Tokolamu's the largest island in this group here. Roughly eight hundred and fifty kilometres north-west of New Zealand. It's been a Department of Conservation nature reserve for some years now and is the hub of an important kiwi breeding programme.'

Jet nodded. He was listening. Or trying to. The projected flight time was echoing in his brain, however. He was going to be cocooned in a flying bubble with Becca as his only companion for *four* hours?

She had to be as unhappy about that prospect as he was.

'Island's area's approximately twenty-six square kilometres and the buildings are located here, in this southern bay.'

Surely there was someone else who could step in and fly the bird?

'Currently there's a group of eighteen people on the island for weed control, checking predator traps and tracking and monitoring the kiwis. All but four of them were in the hostel when the island got rocked by an earthquake, measuring 8.3 on the Richter scale, three hours ago.'

'Where were the other four?'

'Night tracking mission. Common practice, with kiwis being nocturnal feeders.'

'Are they accounted for?'

'No.'

'Any update on the injured people we know about?'

'The hostel got flattened. Three people are still trapped in the debris. Of the rest, there's one with a head injury who's unconscious and another with a compound leg fracture. Radio contact is patchy, however, and we haven't had an update for a while.'

So there were potentially major casualties and the number was still unknown. A lot for a single medic to stabilise and monitor until backup arrived but that was fine. Jet thrived on exactly these kinds of challenges and it wasn't as though he would have to worry about enemy fire this time.

Or would he?

He couldn't help glancing over his shoulder again. Until he arrived on scene, his life would be in the hands of the pilot and in this instance he wasn't at all sure he was comfortable about that. But he'd be even more uncomfortable if he was unprofessional enough to suggest a replacement. Personal issues were simply put aside in his line of work. They were irrelevant.

But this was…different.

He was looking directly at Becca for the first time since he'd entered this room. Making eye contact, and it was doing something very odd to his gut. So many questions were coming out of nowhere.

How are you?

What on earth made you become a pilot?

Do you still miss Matt as much as I do?

Questions he had no right to ask and would probably not get answered.

She was his pilot, dammit. A glorified taxi driver given that her only role was to get him to the island. Transporting patients would have to wait until the navy vessel got to the area and the men around him were discussing just how long that would be. Two days at the earliest. Three, probably, given the weather and sea conditions at the moment.

She wouldn't be there on the island with him so why did this feel personal enough to threaten his performance? She must have wanted this mission. Had she volunteered for it or been chosen and happy to accept? Either way, it sure didn't look as though she was having second thoughts in the wake of learning the identity of her passenger.

Or was she?

There was something about the tilt of her chin and the guarded expression in her eyes as she stared back at him that was...what, a warning?

The idea that it might be a plea seemed weird. Or maybe not. *He* was the person they wanted on this island, after all, and any pilot on this team would be skilled enough to make sure he got there safely. If he demanded a change, it might cause a few waves but it could probably be achieved. How long would it take to put those extra tanks in and connect up the manual fuel lines? Long enough to brief another pilot?

Was that what Becca wanted from him? The opportunity for something rather different and potentially more dangerous than usual?

He'd once been a part of having something desperately important taken away from her. The notion that he could give her anything at all was touching something very deep inside Jet.

It didn't matter that she hated him. She was Matt's sister and whatever she needed or wanted that was within his capability to provide, it was hers, without question.

What *he* needed and wanted was to break that eye contact. To get this mission kicked off and get firmly onto professional territory where he wouldn't have to be aware of this odd stirring in his gut. The one that was making it so hard to look away and was still firing off questions he felt compelled to ask that had absolutely nothing to do with what he was here for.

As luck would have it, he got assistance. A new arrival in the room got everyone's attention instantly. Dressed in the oil-spattered overalls of a mechanic, he gave Becca a thumbs-up sign.

'Tanks are in. You're good to go.'

The interruption was a godsend.

Becca could have sworn she'd been drowning under Jet's gaze. He'd known he had the power to get her bumped off this mission and he'd seen that she wanted it.

And he was prepared to give her what she wanted despite any personal cost involved.

The weird prickling sensation at the backs of her eyes couldn't possibly be tears. Becca didn't cry. Her lifetime supply of tears had been used up ten years ago. It was relief, that was all, and her eyes were more than dry as she took her leave while Jet was to be given the last of his briefing.

They were sparkling, in fact. She had a pre-flight check to get on with so that she'd have the rotors turning and be ready for lift-off as soon as her passenger left the building. A green light to adventure. A take-off with so much extra fuel on board it would be like handling a bomb. A vast amount of unforgiving ocean to fly over. The longest continuous time in the air she'd ever had in a chopper.

Time with Jet Munroe as the only other living creature for hundreds and hundreds of miles.

OK. That was a bit harder to get her head around, so Becca focussed on her checklist instead.

Master power switch on normal.

Inverter switches both on.

Fuel prime pumps both on and lights extinguished.

The checks were automatic but precise. Fast but thorough. She got as far as checking that the pedestal circuit breakers were all in before something broke out of that mental cage she'd pushed Jet into.

She hated him, yes, but it hadn't always been like that, had it?

Hate was the flip side of love.

And a hate this vehement had to be the flip side of adoration.

A teenage crush.

A desperate desire to be noticed as more than just the kid sister of a member of that elite tribe. The four 'bad boys' of Greystones Grammar school. She'd only been eight years old when she'd first met him, when he'd come home with Matt for a holiday from boarding school. That had been the start of it.

Matt's death had finished it, of course. She'd never wanted to set eyes on Jet again.

Becca armed the emergency light in the helicopter and checked the voltmeter. She fired up the engines and finally watched the rotors start to move and pick up speed and height. It was then that the black-clad figure emerged from the hangar door, stooping a little as he came under the rotors to climb into the side door.

Her sigh was unheard, but heartfelt.

Maybe it was true that you should never say never.

CHAPTER TWO

THE ocean was never far away in this island country and the lights of New Zealand's largest city swiftly became a backdrop to the airborne helicopter.

The only communication on board had been between Becca and the mainland. The traffic controller supervised her clearance, confirmed her flight plan and provided a detailed report on weather conditions. For some time after that, the conversation was between others on the ground. Patchy conversations came through about the precise position of the closest ship to the island, the direction it was taking and how long it might be before they reached the island. Confirmation was sought and gained that Becca would be able to refuel using Department of Conservation stores on the island. A worrying update on the condition of the injured people was received and relayed and if it had been possible to fly faster, it would be happening.

With plans in place and the sense of urgency increased, it seemed that any further conversation between anybody was pointless for the time being and, nearly an hour into the flight, the only sound in the cockpit was the roar of powerful engines and the chop of the spinning rotors.

Jet was wearing a helmet with built-in earphones so he could hear whatever was going on. There were open channels to flight control, the helicopter rescue base and the army command in charge of this mission and he'd been taking notice of everything said. Becca could also flip channels so that they could talk to each other without being overheard by anyone else but so far Jet hadn't bothered to pull his microphone attachment down from the rim of his helmet.

He'd been content to listen and simply watch, in no small way amazed that Matt's little sister was doing this at all. Doing it well, too. He had plenty of experience in helicopters. He could fly one himself if he had to, so he could appreciate her skill and the calm control she had over this machine. Just as well, he thought wryly, given that they were carrying enough extra fuel to blow them both to smithereens if something had gone wrong on take-off.

Yep. However unlikely it seemed, Becca Harding had grown up to become a helicopter pilot. Maybe it shouldn't seem so odd. Matt had loved nothing more than getting out with the rest of them and pushing his body and a big bike to the limits. Or was that one of the things that had created the bond between them? The knowledge that Matt didn't have quite the same bravado and that his courage was tested every time? Part of Jet had been impressed. Another part had wanted to watch over him like a big brother and make sure that nothing bad happened.

But something bad had happened, hadn't it?

Jet pushed the accusation back where it had come from with a ruthless mental shove but that only seemed to send other things bubbling to the surface. An image of the small girl he'd met, way back when he'd gone home with Matt for a school holiday. A lonely child being raised by very wealthy and largely absentee parents. Another from years later when they had all stopped in for a day or two at the country mansion on a road trip. More specifically, the memory was the absolute admiration and adoration on a teenage girl's face as she saw her much older brother after too long apart. And the memory that had been captured unwillingly the next day when she had joined them in the swimming pool in her bikini and more than just his brain had taken note that she was no longer a child.

Holy cow! That particular memory had been buried with enough shame to ensure it never escaped. What was happening to him? Jet's scowl deepened as he slumped into his harness, letting minute after minute tick past. Given the roar of engine noise, it was amazing how the atmosphere in this cockpit was starting to feel like a brooding silence. How the tension was ratcheting upwards.

It was ten years ago! It hadn't been his fault, any more than it had been Max's or Rick's. They'd blamed themselves, of course. Especially him, because he'd been the one to have the hunch that Matt's headache wasn't just a hangover hanging on too long. He'd been the one to earn an ED consultant's wrath, arguing that a CT was justified despite the lack of any real symptoms. They had been such junior doctors then—already branded as being brilliant but maverick. None of them had been able to juggle rosters to keep an eye on Matt when he'd decided he'd go to an on-call room and sleep it off.

And it had been Jet who'd gone to try and rouse him, hours later. Nobody had argued about the CT being needed after that. The horror of finding him and learning that a brain aneurysm had ruptured as he slept would never go away completely. Or the pain of being shut out for the next few days as Matt's parents tried to cope with his grief-stricken sister and make agonising decisions about organ donation and turning off the life support.

They'd gone over and over it so many times. They'd made peace with it. He shouldn't have to go through it all again. Shouldn't have to be even thinking about it. It was Becca's fault. For being here. For still hating him.

How much longer was this ride going to last? Jet reached to touch the GPS screen and get an update on what distance had been covered.

'Hands off,' Becca growled. 'I'm the only person who touches the controls in here.'

'Whoa...' Jet drawled, his hand now in a 'stop' signal of mock surrender.

Another minute of an even more tense atmosphere. He sighed inwardly and then flipped his microphone into place as he slid a sideways glance at Becca.

'What if you pass out or something? You expect me to hurtle to my doom even when I'm perfectly capable of handling a BK117?'

Becca was staring straight ahead, as though she was driving a car and needed to keep her eyes on the road. A jerk of her head said that the notion was too farfetched to be worth commenting on.

'You want information, you ask,' she said. 'My bird. My rules.'

Man, she sounded tough. Jet would normally find that worthy of respect but this was *Becca* and the image she was presenting jarred with what he remembered of her. Especially the last time he'd seen her, a few weeks before her brother's death, at a party hosted by the four of them in the old house they'd rented together. Becca had just arrived in the city to start her nursing degree.

An eighteen-year-old, glowing with the excitement of launching herself into the adult world. She'd been all dressed up and ready to party with rings on her fingers and killer heels on her toes. Her hair had been a wild cascade of curls that bounced on her bare shoulders and she had even smelled…*amazing*.

The effect of witnessing this butterfly girl emerging into womanhood had been absolutely riveting. Matt hadn't missed the way Jet's jaw had dropped.

'Don't even go there in your *head*,' his mate had growled. 'You're the prime example of the kind of guy I intend to keep my kid sister well away from.'

The warning had been tempered with a good-natured grin and a friendly punch on the shoulder but it had been serious enough to cause a flash of fear later that night. When Matt had almost walked in on what had happened in the kitchen…

Oh…man. Did *that* memory have to surface again now, as well?

Of course it did. It had never been buried all that well, had it?

Jet had to break this train of thought. He sent a sideways glare at the cause of this mental turbulence. Becca was still staring resolutely straight ahead, seemingly confident of being in control. He couldn't even see that much of her head with that helmet on and it was helpful to remember that she was nothing like the way she was in that memory of that party night.

Now her hair was as short as a boy's and, as far as he could tell, she was wearing neither jewellery nor make-up. And what had her boss called her?

Bec.

The shortest, sharpest diminutive of her name possible.

What was wrong with her old nickname? Was Becca too feminine now? Too soft?

What had happened to that girl?

Jet had to swallow hard. As if he didn't know.

And he didn't want to remember, anyway, did he? He hadn't seen this woman in a decade. They were strangers now. Besides, maybe it wasn't so out of character, now that he came to think of it. Jet felt a corner of his mouth lifting. He couldn't help it. He actually snorted with amusement.

'What?' Becca turned towards him. The helmet seemed too big for her and it made her look younger. Her eyes were narrowed and her lips almost pursed with annoyance. 'You have a problem with something? Like the fact that I'm in charge here?'

'Not at all.'

'What's so damn funny, then?'

'It just reminded me of something.'

'What?'

'You. Cheating at Snakes and Ladders.'

'I didn't cheat.'

'No. You just made up your own rules. What was it? Throw an odd number and you got to go up the snakes instead of down?'

'I was eight years old. A lifetime ago.' Her tone was a warning. 'Keep your memories to yourself, OK?'

'My game, my rules,' Jet murmured.

It was probably coincidence that they happened to hit some turbulence at that precise moment but he glared suspiciously at his pilot anyway. He might have no choice about her being in charge right now but he didn't have to like it, did he?

Damn it!

She'd just begun to think that this wasn't going to be so bad after all.

Jet had always been the brooding type. An intrinsic part of the group but inclined to listen more than speak. To be there. Often leading the action, in fact, but fully informed and able to watch everyone else's back at the same time.

Powerful. With an edge of darkness that had intrigued her from the word go. She'd been scared of him on that first meeting, as any eight-year-old kid would have been, but then she'd finally seen him smile and chasing down that rare occurrence had become her mission. Learning that she could tease and coax him, as easily as her big brother, into doing exactly what she wanted—like playing Snakes and Ladders *her* way—had been a bonus.

Becca was checking every single dial and switch on her control panel. Altitude and power. Fuel supply and speed. RPMs of the main and tail rotors. Checks that were only necessary right now due to her desperate attempt to focus on nothing more than the job in hand.

Yeah… It had been going fine while her passenger had been sitting there quietly. She'd been a bit too aware of him, of course. His size and the sheer…maleness he had always emanated. The tension had been noticeable but manageable, as well. Becca was only too happy to put up with a silent, sulky passenger in this particular instance.

But then he'd tried to mess with her controls! He'd almost *smiled*. Made fun of the fact that she was in charge here. He'd even brought up a somewhat embarrassing reminder of her past and taken her back a little too clearly. Good grief, she'd actually *felt* eight years old again for a heartbeat or two.

She hadn't liked it, either. Not one little bit.

Because she didn't want to remember or was it because she didn't want him thinking of her as someone's kid sister any more?

The tight feeling in her chest increased until it was painful to suck in a breath. She wasn't anyone's kid sister any more, was she? And it was *his* fault.

And she really, really didn't want to spend the next couple of hours or so thinking about what life had been like back then and how much she still missed her big brother. It would have been bad enough simply seeing Jet from a distance. Being this close to him and *only* him, miles from anywhere, was almost unbearable. It was opening an old wound that had been too huge to ever heal over completely and the opening process was a threat. There were soft things underneath that scar that had to be protected at all costs.

Memories.

Feelings.

Hopes and dreams.

Her heart.

Maybe he was right to make fun of her being in charge and trying to sound tough.

Maybe it was all a sham.

The patch of turbulence was great. Becca could feel every tiny nuance of the buffeting and hear the changes in engine noise as though her chopper was talking to her. She became absorbed in her flying and found the thrill creeping back. Being so connected that she became a part of the machine. Or maybe it was an extension of her body. Whatever. They were aloft. She could see the patchy moonlight catching the whitecaps on the ocean below and they were speeding into the night. The turbulence added just enough to the adrenaline rush of it all and by the time they were back into calm air, Becca had found an inner equilibrium, as well.

It didn't matter what Jet remembered or what he thought of her now. She *was* in charge. Of this chopper and who touched its controls. Of what communication, if any, took place between the people involved in this mission.

Flipping channels, Becca checked in with flight control and with her base. Richard was close to the radio.

'Any update on patient status?' she queried.

'No further communication,' Richard responded. 'The link was patchy and we think we might have lost it.'

'Roger that. Any update from the met office?'

'Aftershocks being recorded. Nothing major.'

'Roger. I'll get back to you when we're closer to target.'

Closing off her outward channel to the mainland, Becca left the internal link open. Just in case she felt like talking to Jet.

Which she didn't.

They had nothing in common other than this mission. If it had been anyone else with her, she'd be practically grilling him about what it was like to be part of an elite group like the SAS. What kind of training they got and where they'd been. She would have soaked up every story she could extract and revelled in vicarious dangers. But to ask anything would be opening a Pandora's box with Jet. She'd end up getting filled in on what he'd been doing for the past ten years. She'd probably hear about Max and Rick, as well, and she had to stay away from those connections to the past.

She didn't want to hear about how close they would still be with each other. That whole 'bad boy' vibe that had been a secret pact and bond that she'd been so in awe of. Good grief, she'd actually taken up nursing simply to stay in their orbit. All of them had been special but Matt and Jet had stood out, of course. So different from each other but way too much alike in the power they'd had over her.

The power to be the centre of the universe. Trustworthy and indestructible.

Yes. She had to stay away from it to protect

herself. Because she knew now that it wasn't true. That it was just an illusion.

She had to focus on the present. That fact that she and Jet had nothing in common but this mission. She would take him to the island, drop him off and then fly out of his life and probably never see him again.

Her salvation lay in that, she realised. Or was it a bad idea to break the silence that had filled in such a good chunk of time now? She could be professional but distant. Discussing the mission might be vastly preferable to sitting in a verbal desert for hours and fighting the pull into the past.

'How much do you know about Tokolamu island?' The question came out abruptly, almost an accusation of ignorance. No wonder Jet's eyebrow rose.

'As much as I need to know.' The tone was laid back enough to be a drawl. 'It's the tip of a volcano that could erupt at any time. There are people on top of it who need to get off.'

His voice was right in her ears. As dark and

deep as everything else about this man. That mix of being offhand and supremely confident was him all over, too. A lot of people would find that insufferable rather than attractive.

Maybe she was one of them.

'Some of those people are hurt,' Jet continued. 'It's my job to look after them. Your job is to get me there.'

Yep. She was one of them. Arrogance, that's what it boiled down to.

'Tokolamu's more than just the tip of a volcano,' she informed him. 'It's a significant nature reserve. It's got about seventy species of birds on or around it and that includes a successful breeding programme for endangered kiwi.'

The grunting sound indicated minimal interest but the conversation was working for Becca. Impersonal. Safe.

'There's weka there, too. And even kakapo. Did you know they're the world's heaviest parrot?'

'Can't say I did.'

'They're also the only flightless and nocturnal parrot in existence.'

'Flightless, huh?'

'Yep.'

'They'd be mates with the kiwis, then?'

It was Becca's turn to make a vaguely disparaging sound. Was he putting her down again?

'Well, I reckon the other sixty-eight or so species of bird must think they're a bit inferior.' There was something more alive in Jet's tone now. 'When did you decide you wanted to fly, Becca?'

Becca. Nobody called her that these days. She was Rebecca to people who didn't know her well and Bec to her closer associates. A short, firm kind of name. No frills. Just the way she liked it.

So why did he make it sound like that was her *real* name? As though everyone else, including herself, had been using the wrong one all these years? She shook the disturbing notion away and latched on to his query with relief.

'Ages ago. When I left nursing I went into the ambulance service. They needed an extra crew member on a chopper one night and I got picked. I'd only been up in the air for ten minutes when

I realised I didn't want to be sitting in the back. I wanted the driver's seat.'

Oh…help. This was exactly what she hadn't wanted to be doing. Raking over the past. Divulging far more about herself than she'd intended to. Opening doors that had to remain shut or they would both be sucked into the worst space of all.

Jet's chuckle was so unexpected, her head swung to face him. The sound was more than one of amusement. It signalled sympathy. It said he understood. That he would have felt exactly the same way.

And that was when Becca remembered how he'd got his nickname. Not because his hair was jet black but because he'd had a passion for fast things. Motorbikes and cars. Aircraft. Even his women had to be sleek and ready to speed into his bed.

Hadn't part of his attraction been that he'd had the aura of the kind of things associated with flying? Things like turbulence and danger. The thrill of feeling weightless and able to move with a freedom that could be pure bliss. Maybe the rush she got from flying was the best substitute she had ever been able to discover for how she'd once felt being close to Jet. Being the focus of his attention. Being close enough to accidentally touch.

Not that such a ridiculous notion had ever occurred to her during the process of falling in love with flying and chasing the dream of becoming a pilot. Why would it? She'd never seen Jet again. She'd never been reminded of what it felt like to be this close.

Her sigh was an admission of defeat. She couldn't fight this. She might have lasted amazingly so far, given the distance they had already covered, but she couldn't continue to keep this time together totally impersonal and safe. She had no choice but to face up to whatever emotional fallout eventuated. She had to deal with it and survive. She could do that. She'd done it before, hadn't she?

'So, when did you get your pilot's licence, Jet?'

It was the first time she'd used his name. It

curled off her tongue and hung between them like a white flag of surrender.

'I didn't.'

'I thought you said you could handle a BK.'

'I can. Through osmosis, to start with. Then I got to be mates with some army pilots. They were happy to bend the rules sometimes. And I learn fast.'

That was true enough. Of all the 'bad boys', Jet had undoubtedly been the smartest. That was why he'd won the scholarship to attend an elite, private school in the first place.

'The formal endorsement of the ability was a bit out of my price range,' Jet added dryly.

Yeah…not only the smartest. Despite all those boys being sent to boarding school for reasons they'd had every right to resent, Jet had had the biggest chip on his shoulder about his background. The others, including Matt, had been there because they had parents who could afford to offload the responsibility of children they weren't particularly interested in. It had been years before Becca had learned of Jet's multiple foster-family background. That he'd thought of himself as a charity case. She'd never heard more than hints, however. It wasn't a topic ever up for discussion, any more than the blatant disparity in financial advantages.

Was that why he'd thrown it at her now? As some kind of barrier?

It was ancient history, surely. He'd proved how well he could do relying entirely on his own resources. Becca had a lack of patience for people who blamed life's disappointments on their backgrounds. If you let either the pain of the past or fear of the future dictate your life, you were just shooting yourself in the foot as far as ever being happy. When it came down to it, everybody had to be able to draw on personal strength, no matter what their childhood had been like. Maybe Jet needed to get over himself.

'Med school's not cheap,' she fired back. 'You managed that, no problem.'

'Unless you count the past ten years I've spent paying the loan off.' Jet was scowling but then he shrugged. His next words were barely more than a mutter, as though he was talking to himself rather than Becca. 'Maybe I will get my licence now. It's not as if I want to save up for a house or anything.'

'Gypsy lifestyle, huh?'

Becca regretted her choice of words as soon as she'd uttered them. It was supposed to be a light-hearted comment, to finish the discussion without adding more substance to that ghostly barrier coming into view. To make his life choices seem desirable, even. But the idea of a gypsy was a little too apt. A man going his own way in life, according to his own rules. A bit dark and dangerous. Yes, she could picture Jet Munroe as a gypsy all right. Or a pirate. Or... This had to stop.

'I know what you mean about the osmosis,' she said hurriedly. 'I reckon I could get an IV line in, if push came to shove.'

'I should hope so. Didn't you say you'd been with the ambulance service?'

'I didn't get quite that far with my training.' Becca knew she sounded defensive but did he have to make her sound inadequate? Was he determined to make her feel younger and far less experienced than she was? 'I work with a lot of intensive care paramedics who are brilliant at what they do,' she added crisply. 'My job is just to get them there.'

That seemed to score a point. Conversation ceased and they flew on with the engine noise filling the space. Like it had done a while back but this time it was different. It was like they were both unwillingly forced to be taking part in some kind of dance, Becca decided. They'd drawn closer. Touched on some level. And now they were wheeling apart. Circling. Knowing that they would be drawn in again and next time it would be even closer. Acceptance of the inevitability didn't lessen the dread so Becca said nothing. She was hanging on. Trying to delay the inevitable.

Jet seemed to be in tacit agreement with the tactic. It became a challenge. Who was going to break first? The time stretched and the challenge grew. A distraction all on its own. In the end, it wasn't either of them who broke it. The radio crackled and buzzed inside their helmets. Someone was trying to contact them but reception was bad. Becca switched frequencies and tested them.

'Flight zero three three. Are you receiving me, over?'

On her third attempt, Richard's voice was cracked but audible. They were clearly far enough away from base to be pushing the boundaries for communication and static was wiping out chunks of the speech they could hear.

'…return to base…'

'Please repeat,' Becca said. 'Message broken.'

'…in seismic activity…'

Good grief, had the volcano erupted? No. Becca looked up from the radio controls to stare into the darkness ahead. They were easily close enough by now to see the glow from such an event in the night sky. A sky that was lightening perceptibly with a faint line defining the horizon. Dawn was not that far off and that was good. It would make landing on the island a lot safer.

'…wind shear in the event of eruption,' came the end of Richard's latest broadcast.

So it hadn't erupted, then. Even better.

'…ash…' The single word was another warning.

'Message broken,' Becca said again.

'…pager…' The word was a command now. '…mobile…'

'Roger. Over and out.'

They flew in silence again for a minute. And then another. Becca was reluctant to follow the instruction. Even as broken as the communication had been, it was clear the mission was in danger of being aborted. And they were almost there, dammit. With no obvious cause for alarm.

'You going to check your pager, then?' Jet queried. 'And your phone?'

'Yep.'

Another minute passed. The sky was definitely getting lighter. Becca peered ahead. Was it too soon to expect to make visual contact with Tokolamu?

'Any time soon?' Jet murmured.

With a sigh, Becca unclipped the pager from her belt and handed it to her passenger. He activated the device and started scrolling through messages.

'These seem to be old messages. When did you go to Cathedral Cove?'

'Yesterday. About eleven hundred hours. Idiot teenagers diving off the cliff into some big waves. One of them mistimed it and got banged up on the rocks. Winch job.'

'And south of the Bombay Hills?'

'That was the job before Cathedral Cove. Motorway pile-up.'

'Nothing new on here, then.'

'I'm not surprised. Range for the radio should be better than the pager.'

'Give me your phone.'

The reluctance to let Jet read any text message she might have was surprisingly strong but Becca shrugged it off. It wasn't as if there would be anything too personal in there. Like a message from a boyfriend. She almost wished there was. She could be sure that Jet's love life wasn't a desert and her single status would probably be enough to count as another putdown. Or was some of this feeling of inadequacy coming from something she'd considered long since buried? She wasn't old enough. Or special enough. She was just Matt's kid sister and Jet was…

'Here it is. It says "Cancel, cancel. Seismic activity increasing. Eruption considered imminent. Risk unacceptable. Return to base."'

'No.'

'What?' But there was something more than astonishment in Jet's tone. It sounded like admiration. Respect, even.

'Look.' Becca pointed, and Jet peered into the grey sky of early dawn. 'Two o'clock,' she added.

Lumpy shapes that weren't waves. Getting larger by the second. The chain of islands of which Tokolamu was the largest. Becca could see it clearly now. Could see the tip of the volcano and it was as dark as the rest of the rocky land mass.

'We haven't got the fuel to get back,' she said calmly. 'Personally, I'd rather take my chances after a safe landing on an island than ditching in the ocean somewhere.'

There was a moment's silence as Jet absorbed the implications. Becca finally turned to look at him and, to her amazement, he grinned at her.

'Your bird,' he said. 'Your rules.'

His face was really alive now. Dark eyes gleamed beneath the visor of the helmet. They were breaking the rules and hurling themselves towards danger and he was loving it. And…oh, Lord…that smile could probably persuade her to do anything, however dangerous it obviously was.

Maybe she should turn back. There was a life raft on board. They would know their coordinates and another chopper could possibly already be on the way to meet them.

But the islands were so close now. She could think about spotting the buildings and then locating the nearby landing site. People desperately needed the assistance she was bringing. If she got stuck on the island because an ash cloud prevented take-off then so be it. It wasn't as though—

The oath Jet breathed cut off any thought of potential safety.

Had she really thought the sky was so light now? Against the glow of an erupting volcano, it had gone pitch black again.

Ash would kill the engines. How long before it enveloped them? Becca began dropping altitude. Heading for the closest island. Except that was Tokolamu, wasn't it? And maybe it wasn't ash she had to worry about first. The force of the eruption was about to hit them. Wind shear would drop them like a rock…

It *was* dropping them. Becca was fighting with the controls of her machine and she knew it was pointless. So pointless she didn't say a thing when she found Jet leaning in to try and take over. She couldn't hear a thing he was shouting because the noise outside was overwhelming everything. The sky was on fire and the island and its surrounding sea was rushing towards them so fast she could barely process the information.

She was about to die and Jet Munroe was trying to save her.

The irony of the situation barely registered before the cacophony of sound and light around her vanished and everything became black.

CHAPTER THREE

HE WAS fighting for his life.

For Becca's life, too. Man, that look on her face was pure determination without a hint of fear. She was so small and fierce and seemed to believe that she could wrestle the force of Mother Nature and an out-of-control aircraft into submission.

The impression would have been laughable if it hadn't been so incredibly fleeting. Shoved aside with a million other, irrelevant thoughts as Jet let an automatic part of his brain loose. The part that stored emergency procedures backed up by remarkably honed survival skills.

Even so, in that mental maelstrom he recognised another motive to win this challenge. Maybe he had to do this for Matt. It was too late to save his best mate but he could save the person who'd been so important to him. The small, lonely girl that he'd tried so hard to be a substitute parent to. As well as a big brother and best friend all at the same time. Matt would have given his life in a heartbeat to save his sister.

Jet could do no less.

Except…they weren't going to die, dammit. Not if he could do anything about it. He added his weight to Becca's to fight the controls and, for a split second the sickening downward spiral lessened and he could see straight ahead. Towards the foam of waves breaking on unforgiving black rocks. And past the rocks to a tiny area of shingle beach. Would solid land be a better option than an icy ocean and the pull of its current?

Not that he really had much choice in the matter but the instantaneous, clinical evaluation of potential options filled those last few seconds before speed, gravity and the total failure of this machine to respond well enough combined and they hit…*something*. Hard.

Hard enough to knock him out?

He couldn't be sure. His head was spinning,

filled with a roaring sound and bright flashes of light. He could be regaining consciousness after God knew how long or…this could be moments after the crash and the window in which he could escape.

And survive.

Something overrode that pure survival instinct, however. The knowledge that he hadn't been alone.

'Becca… *Becca…*'

He couldn't see anything. Couldn't open his eyes. Something was digging painfully into his face and it took a moment to realise that the pain was caused by broken pieces of his flight helmet visor. He wrenched them clear and pulled his helmet off, ignoring the warm, sticky sensation of bleeding.

Now he could see surprisingly well. Red light, like a fiery dawn, surrounded them. The Perspex of the helicopter was cracked and a horribly bent rotor blade was directly in front, framed by a large hole. A spray of water suddenly came through the hole and soaked him, cold enough to wake him up completely. Were they in the sea? No. He could feel something solid beneath them and the crumpled chassis of the chopper was rocking. Grinding on something hard.

The rocks. They must be caught on rocks, probably close to dry land. A wave could lift the wreckage and put it at the mercy of the ocean at any moment and that wouldn't be a good thing. The spray had barely stopped but Jet had released his harness and his attention was focussed on the crumpled body of his pilot.

'*Becca.* Can you hear me?'

The groan that came in response was the best sound Jet had ever heard.

She was alive.

Stripping off the gloves he'd been wearing, Jet moved to wedge himself between what was left of the Perspex bubble and a flight control panel that was bent and broken. A couple of faint, flickering lights caught his attention as he moved. Hopefully, one of them might be the emergency locator beacon activating. The other one was on the radio and, on the off chance it was still operational, Jet pulled on the curly microphone cord to wrench it clear of the central controls it had fallen into.

'Mayday, mayday,' he sent. 'Flight zero zero three down.'

Even if they got the message, they wouldn't be sending another rescue chopper. Flying into volcanic ash was impossible. The only hope of assistance would come from the ship already diverted towards Tokolamu and, what had they said about its ETA?

Thirty-six hours. A day and a half.

They were on their own.

Apart from another group of survivors on this island who still needed help, of course. Jet depressed the button on the side of the microphone again.

'Abandoning aircraft,' he said decisively. If this transmission was getting through, at least nobody would waste time trying to search the crash site later. 'We'll head for the settlement.'

A faint crackle emanated from the radio then another spray of salt water came through the windscreen and the electronic equipment fizzed and died. He had wasted no more than about thirty seconds on what was probably a useless attempt to communicate with the outside world but it still felt like way too long.

Becca needed him.

Dropping the microphone, Jet used his hands and eyes to try and examine her. These weren't the worst conditions under which he'd done a primary survey on an injured person but they were nudging the top spot. He could feel the wash of the waves around the helicopter chassis and getting sucked out to sea and then smashed onto rocks again would be pretty much as dangerous as being under enemy fire.

Airway. Breathing. Circulation.

Becca groaned more loudly and mumbled some incomprehensible words but the attempt to speak was a good indication that her airway was clear. Breathing? Jet put his hands around her ribs, oblivious of the fact that he was cupping her breasts as he concentrated on what was happening below her ribs. Were her lungs filling well? The same amount on each side? Was her breathing too fast or too slow? God, she was so small.

Fragile.

Her breathing seemed OK. Jet ran his hands over the rest of her body. Feeling her abdomen to see if it elicited a pained response. Checking her legs for the deformity of a broken bone or the wetness of major bleeding. Amazingly, he found nothing. Until he checked her arms, anyway. When he felt her left arm below the elbow, Becca cried out and opened her eyes.

'It's OK,' he told her. 'You've hurt your arm.'

Broken it, quite likely, because of how hard she'd been gripping the controls at the point of impact. Her flight suit was ripped and she was bleeding badly. Jet ripped the sleeve farther and tied the strips tightly over the wound. There was no time to do more right now. This first check might have only taken sixty seconds but it was past time to get out of there.

'Becca? Can you hear me?'

Her eyes opened but she said nothing.

'Does your neck hurt?'

Her head rolled from side to side but she still made no sound.

'Can you move your feet?'

He felt rather than saw the attempt at movement because he was busy easing her helmet off and unclipping her harness. The queries had been automatic, anyway. Even if she did have serious neck or spinal injuries, he had to get her out.

The door on the pilot's side was crunched against solid rock. They were tilted slightly nose down and another huge rock was blocking the door on the passenger side. That left the side door in the cabin and the back hatch under the tail. One of those was bound to provide an escape route but it would take precious seconds to get there. A wave rolled them enough to lift the tail and knock him off balance even as he considered the options.

Becca's eyes were wide open and well illuminated by the eerie, red glow from the outside. Could she hear the frightening roar of the volcanic eruption that was almost enough to cover the horrible grinding of metal on rock? She was clearly putting the pieces together and starting to realise what had happened and where they were.

He saw the moment that fear kicked in.

A new surge of adrenaline came with the renewed urge to protect Becca. Turning and bracing himself on the back of the seat, Jet used his heavy, steel-capped boots to smash the edges of the hole in the Perspex to make it bigger. Big enough to climb out of with a small woman in his arms.

The world had turned itself inside out. It was threatening to crush her and there was nothing Becca could do about it.

She hadn't felt this afraid since…

Since the moment she had known Matt was going to die.

Nobody had taken her into his arms back then and held her as though he was capable of keeping the chaos and pain away.

Maybe this was simply an illusion now but if she was going to die, Becca would far rather be cradled in a pair of powerful arms that made it feel like her life was of the utmost importance to someone else than curled up alone in the pilot's seat of a crashed helicopter.

She'd obviously been knocked out on impact and the memories of her last moments of consciousness were patchy and strange. So was what she could remember about waking up.

Jet's hands on her breasts. Pressing on her abdomen. Tracing the shape of her whole body.

She'd known they were *his* hands. She'd always known what it would feel like to have them touching her because it had happened in so many, many dreams. It was muted in reality, however, because in those dreams her skin had always been bare.

The pain of having her arm moved had chased any pleasure away. It had woken her up too much, as well. Enough to make sense of where she was and what was happening. To realise that the weird red light was a reflection that had to be coming from molten lava spewing from a very nearby volcano. To feel how unstable the remains of this helicopter were and that it was seawater splashing inside at regular intervals to pool around her feet.

Fear overrode any pain at that point and only increased as she watched Jet kick the remnants of Perspex from in front of them. He was going to escape, wasn't he? The way he had when Matt had been lying there dying in the intensive care unit. She would have to cope alone again and she was so horribly, horribly afraid.

But then he bent over and gathered her into his arms. She was rocked wildly as he completed the enormously difficult manoeuvre of climbing through a hole with jagged edges, holding such a large burden, trying not to get them caught or injured. Then there were sharp, slippery rocks to negotiate and Jet had to use one hand to steady himself every few seconds. Somehow, he still managed to hold Becca with one arm. She could feel it across her back and tucked under her thighs like the sturdy branch of a tree. Maybe it was helping that she'd wound her arms around his neck and had her face buried against his shoulder.

A roaring noise surrounded them that was far more than the sound the sea could make against rocks. The ground shook beneath them at intervals, as well. How on earth did Jet manage to keep them moving? Upright enough to avoid a nasty fall on this alien landscape of ancient, volcanic rock. Becca clung to him as tightly as she could. She fought hard when something threatened to prise her arms loose.

'Let go.' Jet's voice was a command. 'It's all right. It's safe now.'

Reluctantly, Becca let him unwind her arms. He was kneeling, she realised with surprise, and she was sitting on a flat area of shingle, having been deposited so carefully she hadn't noticed.

She looked around cautiously. Good grief…they could be on Mars. A lurid red sky and barren dark rocks were the only things she could see until she lifted her line of sight. And there, well out on the rocks, cradled in a wash of sea foam, she could see the sad wreckage of her beautiful chopper.

'Oh, my God,' she breathed, wrapping her arms

around herself for comfort as the enormity of the situation became suddenly very real.

'Give me your arm.'

'What?' Becca stared at Jet in confusion. He'd just removed her arms from where she'd been clinging to him like a frightened child.

An eight-year-old, maybe? How did he do it? Strip away all her skills and hard-won strength to make her feel so incredibly vulnerable. And lost now. She couldn't pretend to be in control any more. She hadn't protected herself very well, had she?

She hadn't protected either of them. This was *her* fault. She could have turned back. She'd risked her life, which was bad enough, but she'd also risked Jet's life and that was…appalling. And he was hurt. There was blood on his face. Without thinking, Becca reached up to touch. The urge to find out how bad it was…to make it better somehow…was too powerful to resist.

'No.' Jet pushed her away. 'Your left arm.' He was leaning closer. Frowning. 'Where are you?' he demanded.

He didn't want her to touch him. Weird how much that hurt. 'H-here,' Becca stammered, confused again. 'With you.'

'Fair enough.' There was a curl happening to one corner of his mouth. Almost a smile. 'You got knocked out, Becca,' he said with a curiously gentle note in his voice. 'I'm trying to assess your GCS. Can you tell me where "here" is?'

'The island. Tokolamu.'

'Good. And what's my name?'

'Jet.' Becca said it slowly because it felt good. Like permission to go somewhere she had been denied access to for so long.

'My real name?'

'James Frederick Munroe.'

'*Ouch!* How on earth did you remember my middle name?'

Becca felt herself grin. 'I remember lots of things.'

What an understatement, a part of her brain chided. Did you really think you'd locked all that stuff away? It's still there. Every detail. The way he could scowl so fiercely whenever anything remotely emotional was happening. The astonishing intensity of his dark eyes when he was interested in something. The way his hair looked when sleekly wet coming up from a dive into a swimming pool, or damp and tousled by a towel after a shower. The way he'd sat with a small child and played Snakes and Ladders when he could have been doing far more exciting teenage stuff like playing video games or raiding her parents' well-stocked liquor cabinet. The dreams that had started a long, long time before any sexual content had crept in.

Dreams that had only gained momentum the night of the party.

The excitement of dressing up like an adult. Of finally being grown up enough to…

To have no hesitation at all in grabbing that opportunity when she'd been alone in the kitchen with Jet when they'd both gone to find a drink at the same time. When they'd been side by side in the narrow space between the open fridge door and the wall.

When she had turned and kissed him.

She could still remember that moment when their lips had actually touched. The sheer *bliss* of it…

And then there'd been the sound of her brother coming down the hallway. Calling out to Jet to see why the beer was taking so long to arrive. And Jet had let her go and turned so fast he had practically been on a fridge shelf by the time Matt came into the room seconds later.

And he hadn't even looked at her once for the rest of that night.

Her grin was fading as rapidly as Jet had dismissed her way back then. Pandora's box had been split wide open. During the crash? No. The cracks had been apparent the moment she'd seen Jet step out of that vehicle at the base. It had only been a matter of time before the contents began to spill out. There was so much of it, how could it all be appearing with such speed? Maybe it would be helpful to hang on to the devastation that had come in the wake of being ignored after taking the risk of that kiss.

Jet was just registering the mischievous grin

that had already vanished. He gave an impatient huff. 'Your retrograde memory is too good. OK, remember these things coz I'm going to ask you again in five minutes. A brown dog, the number six and the name Reginald. Which is marginally better than Frederick,' he added wryly. 'Now, let me see your arm. It was bleeding.'

He'd tied a makeshift kind of tourniquet around it, she noticed. No wonder he was checking her level of consciousness. She had no memory of him ripping the sleeve of her flight suit to make the wide bands.

The wound began bleeding heavily as soon as the bands were loosened.

'Needs stitching,' Jet muttered.

Becca saw her own blood covering his hands as he examined her arm. She was horrified.

'You're not wearing any gloves.'

His raised eyebrows that framed a very intent look. 'Something you want to tell me?' He made a tutting sound. 'What *have* you been up to, Rebecca Harding?'

He was teasing her. Just the way he had when

she'd been a kid and had come inside with grazed knees or muddy clothes. Only this was about a very adult subject. Becca had been shivering with the cold but could feel heat suffusing her face right now.

'N-nothing.' Unfortunately true but did he really have to know how sad her love life had been for so long? Did she need current humiliation to add to a long-ago memory? Definitely not.

'Not recently, anyway,' she added in what she hoped was an offhand tone. 'Don't worry. You're not going to catch any blood-borne nasty. It's just not good practice, is it?'

Jet probably saw right through her small attempt to get a grip on things.

'Least of our worries right now, I would've thought.' He had retied the strips of the dense, waterproof fabric. 'Wriggle your fingers for me.'

The attempt wasn't impressive.

'Hurts, doesn't it?'

Becca shrugged. 'A bit. I'll be fine. What's happened to *your* head? You're bleeding, too.'

He wasn't going to be distracted from his careful examination of her wrist and arm. He bent her hand carefully.

'Ouch,' Becca muttered.

'Could be broken,' he pronounced. 'Could just be a bad sprain. I'll put a compression bandage on when I've sorted that bleeding. Anything else hurting?'

'No.'

'Really?' His gaze narrowed. 'No headache?'

'A bit, I guess.'

'What were the three things I told you to remember?'

'A brown dog…number six and the name…' The urge to tease was childish. Or maybe she couldn't resist seeking the same kind of rapport he might have been trying to tap into when he'd been chiding her about her possible sex life. '…Frederick,' she said decisively.

She held his gaze. Jet sighed heavily but she was sure she'd seen a gleam of appreciation there at her feeble attempt to lighten the atmosphere.

'Don't move. I'm going to get my kit.'

'What? Where is it?'

'In the chopper. Along with a lot of other useful medical gear I should try and retrieve. We've still got an appointment with some injured people who can't be too far away.'

'But…' Becca looked past him. The light was stronger now. A little less red maybe but no less strange. The air looked thick. With ash? She didn't know much about volcanoes but surely they'd need to find some kind of masks to breathe through?

The helicopter wreckage was clearly visible, a bent rotor sticking up in the air like a distressed swimmer's arm. The other rotor seemed to be wedged in the rocks but it wasn't enough of an anchor for stability. The mortally wounded aircraft was rolling with each wave. Tipping and sliding on the rocks.

'You can't go back inside,' she told Jet. 'It's far too dangerous.'

But Jet was standing up.

What if something happened to him? If he got trapped inside and the wreckage got sucked off the rocks by an extra-big wave? He'd drown and…and it would be worse than sitting here alone, waiting for a wall of molten lava to swallow her up.

'Don't go… *Please…*'

The words were a whisper but he seemed to have heard them. He crouched swiftly, putting his hands on her shoulders.

'I have to,' he said quietly. 'We need the medical supplies. It won't take long.'

His gaze was holding hers. Was he trying to reassure her? Give her strength?

It wasn't working.

'I'll be right back,' Jet said with absolute confidence. 'I'll look after you, OK?'

Becca nodded but bit her lip at the same time. She shouldn't need looking after. She was a grown-up. A highly trained helicopter pilot. A woman in complete control of her life and her future. At least, she had been, until a very short time ago.

At this precise moment, she was only too grateful to be given that promise. To pull it around her like a comforting hug.

Jet was standing up again. He looked down. His face was half-covered in blood and his expression could only be described as grim but those dark eyes were so alive. Gleaming, in fact.

'We're on land now,' he told her. 'My game. *My* rules.'

And with that, he was gone. A shape so dark and lithe it was only seconds before he virtually vanished against the rocks.

Leaving Becca, huddled alone on that tiny, stony beach, was one of those 'lesser of two evils' decisions.

Jet's head told him that it was what had to be done. He needed his medical gear to help her as well as the other people on this island. What use were his skills if he had no pain relief or fluids or any of the dozens of other things compressed into his specialist backpack? There were items in the helicopter he'd been counting on, as well, but they would have to be left behind. Things like portable oxygen and traction splints and the life pack. There was no point in retrieving anything he wouldn't be able to carry himself.

Part of his brain was pointing out that Becca still had one good arm so she'd be able to carry something but Jet was arguing the notion as he scrambled back over the rocks. He could feel the pain in his hands, despite how cold they were, as he tried to grip the sharp surfaces and he made a mental note to keep an eye out for the leather gloves he'd stripped off in order to feel what he was doing in that first check on Becca's condition.

He'd felt it all right. No amount of mental discipline could shove it all into a doctor-patient box. The relief of finding she wasn't badly injured had warned him of an unprofessional involvement. The wrench of putting her down on the beach had been another warning and even that had paled in comparison to having to leave her behind moments ago, with that look in her eyes.

She had wanted him to stay with her.

She *needed* him.

Jet didn't try and climb directly into the cockpit. Eyeing the hole they had escaped through gave him a moment of satisfaction at the achievement. Would he have even attempted that without the incentive of getting Becca out as fast as possible?

Probably not.

This time, he went around to the back of the aircraft. Cautiously. Allowing a wave to break high on his legs and then ebb before going for the tail hatch. Another wave broke before he managed to get it open and the whole chassis rocked so that he barely kept his grip on the handle. He'd have to be quick about this but that was a good thing. It left no room for fear. Or the distraction of that image of Becca on the beach, looking to him to keep her safe.

His pack was easy enough to find and drag out from where it had wedged itself under the stretcher. He shoved it through the hole in the front with enough force to get it far enough up on the rocks to stay dry. The action made the hole even bigger, which would be good if he had to dive for safety but it was letting a lot more water in at the same time. He was sloshing around almost up to his knees as it was but he took the time to do a swift search in the dim light of the cabin. He grabbed a drug kit and an IV roll and bags of fluids, unzipping the jacket of his suit to tuck them against his body. A whole box of masks. He was adding a handful of extra bandages when the slide of the wreckage on rock tipped him off balance and he barely got himself upright before it moved again.

Without thinking, he snapped the clip holding the life pack in place and clutched it in his arms as he stepped forward and then turned to roll backwards through the same hole through which he'd lifted Becca to safety. His ankle caught and he felt a nasty wrench that wasn't coming simply from his own momentum. The chopper was really moving this time. Far and fast enough to break the rotor blade that had been caught between rocks.

Jet sucked in a breath as he realised that that relatively tiny piece of metal had been all that had kept the chopper where it was. It rolled away now, giving itself up to the sea.

He still had the life pack in his arms and lumpy supplies tucked into his jacket. His pack was safe. Carefully, Jet got to his feet, testing his ankle. It hurt like hell but it could take his weight, thank goodness. He could see that Becca was standing, as well. Staring in his direction. He couldn't see her expression but he could imagine what it was, having just watched her helicopter slide into the sea and probably not aware that he'd rolled to safety. He raised his hand, thumb up, to signal her.

Mission accomplished.

This time, the deep breath he sucked in was a satisfied one. He'd done what he'd set out to do. Showing Becca how capable he was, even in a dangerous situation, felt damn good.

He'd said it wouldn't take long and that he would be back. She would know she could trust him to honour his word.

He would do what he'd promised her he would.

He would look after her.

CHAPTER FOUR

THE sea was the same colour as the sky.

The colour of blood.

The dark silhouette of the man was only recognisable because it moved and the surrounding rocks didn't. When he stood still, having risen and raised his hand in a triumphant fist, he looked like another shape carved in stone.

A human rock.

Becca didn't bother reminding herself that she never cried. That her tears had all been spent on Matt. A choked sob escaped as she realised that, in no small part, this was still about Matt.

Her brother had been her human rock in a fluid, lonely world and Jet had been there beside him for as far back as she could remember clearly. Too real and too powerful to be considered a shadow but he'd still been in the background.

Like a guardian angel. A flesh-and-blood angel with a loyalty that was so absolute it was impossible to think of Matt without thinking of Jet, and vice versa.

So it was like part of her brother was here with her now. Promising to look after her. Expecting her to trust him, but how could she when she knew that that trust could be broken? Unintentionally, maybe, but the effect would be the same and she'd be alone again. In the end, Becca knew she had only herself to rely on with that kind of certainty.

But the pull towards leaning on Jet and giving him that trust was so strong it was a physical pain and that was why Becca was crying now. Maybe, if she hadn't just watched in horror as the wreckage of her aircraft had slipped into that blood-red sea when she had been sure Jet was still inside it, she might have been powerless to resist that pull on her heart. But for just a few of its beats there she'd known how unwise it would be to give Jet any part of her heart, and trusting him would do precisely that.

For those few, ghastly seconds she'd known she was on her own again and she'd known that she *could* survive. She'd done it before and she knew how. She knew that a big part of being able to survive was about dodging emotional as well as physical damage. For however long it would take to get off this island, the man coming towards her now, weighed down by the bulky gear he was carrying, was just as dangerous as the exploding volcano high above them.

'Sorry, this is going to sting like mad.'

'You could just stitch it up. You don't need to waste the local.'

Jet snorted. 'I don't happen to have a bullet handy for you to bite on. Hold still… Damn, this light is still awful.'

'I'm sure you can do this with your eyes shut. Your reputation precedes you with the speed of light. Hey, well done! You're wearing gloves this time.'

Was she mocking him? Jet sent her a suspicious glower but Becca's head was bent. Good grief, she actually wanted to watch him cobbling up this nasty gash on her arm? And she was pre-pared to have it done without the benefit of local anaesthetic?

She had a mask on now. They both did. It was the first thing Jet had sorted, having arrived back on the beach and emptied the extra supplies from inside his jacket, just in case they suddenly got enveloped by an ash cloud. He was perfectly used to being around people wearing surgical masks. He was even used to being in environments where the light was weird due to explosions and smoke and so forth, but Becca had never been in a war zone, as far as he knew. This had to be an extraordinary experience for her, sitting hunched and injured on a beach in the middle of nowhere, bathed in the glow of molten lava and shivering with the cold and probably fear and yet, here she was, managing to keep her arm steady on his knee ready for him to do some minor surgery.

He grunted softly. A sound of respect. 'Pretty tough, aren't you?'

Becca shrugged. 'When I need to be.'

It had to hurt, sliding the needle in deeply enough to numb the edges of this wound. He saw the way she flinched and he could feel it himself. It wasn't that he was ever without sympathy for any patient he was inflicting a painful procedure on but this felt different. Unpleasant enough to make this an ordeal for both of them so it was best he got it done as efficiently as possible.

And he was wearing the damn gloves for her protection, not his.

Waiting only a minute or two for the local to take effect, Jet busied himself sorting the dressing and bandages he'd need. He located his suture materials and some small pouches of saline. Ripping the corner of the first pouch, he tipped the sterile liquid onto the wound. Becca sucked in her breath and Jet winced inwardly.

'Not quite numb, huh?'

'I'm fine,' she said through obviously gritted teeth. 'Just get on with it. We need to get out of here.' She was silent for a moment and when she spoke again, her tone was far less sure. 'Do you think we'll be able to get to the conservation base?'

'May as well give it a go,' Jet said cheerfully. 'Not too much else to do, is there? How much do you know about this volcano?' He was onto the second pouch of saline now, trickling it into the centre of the wound and tipping her arm carefully so that it drained towards the edges.

'What do you mean?'

'I'm wondering how many craters there are, for instance. And whether any of them had lakes.' Having made the wound as clean as possible, Jet swabbed it dry with clean gauze and then ripped open the packet containing the curved suture needle and attached thread. He had to swab fresh bleeding away then and decided it needed a couple of deep stitches before he closed the surface.

Becca looked away as the needle advanced. 'Does it make a difference? Having lakes?'

'Could do. Lakes mean you can get lahars. Rivers of mud and stuff that can do a lot of damage. They can move a lot faster than anyone can run and they set like concrete. They've been known to wipe out entire villages.'

'So we might get to the base camp and find it's too late,' Becca said quietly.

Jet made no response. What was the point? They might not even get there at all but they had to try.

'Lava's not so bad,' he said a short time later, now working swiftly to insert, knot and clip the neat sutures closing the wound. 'Generally moves slowly enough so you can keep out of the way. The problem will be if it's cut access off completely.'

'What about the gases volcanoes give off? Aren't they poisonous?'

'Some of them,' Jet admitted. 'But there's no point worrying about it given that we're a bit limited in what we can do. Staying upright is a good idea because a lot of those gases are heavier than air and will accumulate close to ground level. Respirators would be ideal but I guess we're lucky we've got these good quality antiviral-type masks. If we moisten them, they'll be more effective against gases as well as ash.'

He clipped the final suture and put a sticky, clear dressing over the wound.

'I'll bandage it for now. If it gets any more painful we'll splint it properly. Try not to put too much weight on it.'

'Thanks, Doc. I'll keep that in mind.'

Definitely mocking him now and he probably deserved it. Heaven only knew how rough the journey they were about to undertake might be. Becca might well need to climb up steep cliffs or get down rough gullies. Not using an arm was hardly going to be on a priority list if you were trying to save yourself from further injury.

'I should have kept our helmets on,' he muttered. 'Stupid.'

'I've got sunglasses.' Becca patted a top pocket of her flight suit. 'Have you?'

'Yeah….somewhere, I think.'

'Should help keep ash out of our eyes at least. Mine are starting to sting a bit.'

'Yeah…mine, too.' Jet tore the end of the bandage with his teeth and made strips to tie it in place around Becca's arm. 'There you go. That should hold together a bit better than crocodile clips.' He turned to begin putting unused supplies back into the pack.

'Leave some saline,' Becca ordered. 'And a sticky dressing. And have you got some Steri-strips?'

'What for?' He swung his head back towards her sharply. Was she hurt somewhere else, as well?

'Because you've got a dirty big gash on your forehead, that's why.'

'It can wait.'

'Have you not even noticed how often you're wiping blood off before it can get in your eyes? Quite apart from the risk of infection if it's not covered up, it might be helpful not to get your vision obstructed at some critical point.'

Jet grimaced but had to concede the point. He dampened another gauze dressing and swabbed at his forehead. The fluid stung enough to let him know the gash was not small.

'Give that to me,' Becca ordered. 'You're probably making it worse, scrubbing at it like that.'

With a frustrated growl, Jet sat down and handed the swab over. Becca knelt beside him and peered at his forehead. She was concentrating on the task at hand but she was so close to him that Jet had to drag his gaze away from her face. Not before he noticed how amazingly thick and dark her eyelashes were even without the benefit of mascara, however. Or that her nose was small enough to barely dent the mask. And he hadn't needed X-ray vision to imagine what her lips were like beneath the stiff fabric. Did she still trap the tip of her tongue between them when she was totally focussed, the way she always had as a child?

He could actually sense her body heat in this proximity. Along with the light but confident touch of her fingers, it was disturbing.

'Get on with it,' he muttered. 'We need to get going. Get to higher ground, at least, so we won't be sitting ducks for a lahar.'

'Fine.' Becca used a fresh dressing to dry the

wound. 'This could do with stitching, I expect, but Steri-strips will have to do until you get to an expert. You up to date with a tetanus shot?'

'Yep. Are you?'

'I think so.' Becca was trying to open the vacuum-sealed package containing the small, super-sticky strips. The corner of the plastic side was eluding her because her hands were shaking.

With the cold? Or was she finding this as disturbing as he was?

'Here. Let me.' Closing his hands over hers to take the packet without dropping it, Jet was startled by a blast of heat. How could Becca be shivering with cold when her skin could scorch his with such a brief touch? He had to suck in a deep breath.

He found himself sucking in a flashback at the same time.

That moment behind the fridge door at that party. The kiss.

It had just been a combination of teenage excitement and alcohol. Hadn't it?

She must have known as well as he had how

Matt would have reacted. How impossible it would have been. And she'd been barely old enough for anything other than him being a 'big brother' figure to be remotely acceptable.

Hadn't stopped him thinking about it, though, had it?

Considering the amazing possibility that might be there if Matt ever came around to the idea one day. Thinking about how...*right* it would seem.

But Matt had never guessed his errant thoughts in those last few weeks he'd had to live and if it had been an embryonic dream, it had been buried along with his best mate. He hadn't even thought about it since.

Until now, that was. Jet cleared his throat, hoping to clear the memory, as well.

'You're not wearing gloves,' he managed to say casually as he handed her back the opened packet. 'Tch, tch.'

'Hmm.' Becca pressed an end of a strip to his forehead and then he could feel her squeezing the edges of the wound together to bring the other side close enough to capture. 'And I've probably got more to worry about in that direction than you have.'

Was he imagining an odd note in her voice? Disapproval?

Unless…

Unless there *had* been more to that kiss than too much champagne and being unexpectedly in such close proximity.

Maybe the attraction had been there on both sides.

But, even if it had been, it was ancient history. So long ago it was ridiculous to think it had any relevance now.

She hated him. She had told him that with a vehemence that had been absolute and he had known it would be there for ever. They might have been forced into being this close now but this was about survival. She needed him whether she liked it or not. And he needed her, too. This could potentially be the biggest challenge he'd ever faced and who knew? If it came down to the wire, the extra incentive of his determination to get Matt's little sister to safety might be enough to tip the balance from giving up to being successful.

'I think not,' he said aloud, in as cool a tone as he could manage. 'Thanks to a career in front-line emergency medicine, I get regular checks for any blood-borne nasties, as you call them. I'm as clean as a whistle.'

'Good for you.' The pressure of her fingers was even firmer this time. Enough to hurt. Not that he was going to let her know that. 'And now you'll have a sexy little scar on your head like a pirate. I'm sure it'll add considerably to your pulling power with women.'

The sound of her ripping the backing off a sticky dressing was rather similar to the edge that had definitely been in her tone that time.

Jet couldn't help teasing her. 'Cool,' he murmured. 'I'll be sure to remember to send you a thank-you card.'

She snorted. 'You'll need to get to a post office first.' She stuffed supplies back into a plastic compartment of the pack and zipped it shut. Then she fished her sunglasses from her pocket and put them on, foiling the attempt to read her expression that Jet had been unaware of making. She stood up, her very effectively disguised face pointed down at him. 'Well? What are you still sitting around for? Which way shall we go?'

Jet got to his feet. He opened a side pocket of the pack to extract a heavy-duty 'hazardous waste' plastic bag, which he handed to Becca.

'Make yourself useful,' he ordered. 'Put the extra stuff in there. Those bandages and masks and things.'

He hefted the pack onto his back as she complied. Then he lifted the life pack with one hand and held out his other hand for the bag she had filled.

'I'll take this. I can carry the life pack, as well.'

'What with? Your potentially fractured arm? I don't think so.' Jet was scanning the area, his gaze narrowed and focussed.

The red glow had diminished enough to bleach a lot of the colour from the sea and sky and the daylight was strengthening by the minute, but he could see the glow well enough to pinpoint the location of the eruption. He turned in a three-hundred-and-sixty-degree circle, trying to feel whether there was any wind. Even a small breeze would help keep them safe from the effects of ash or gas if they could move into it. They needed high ground, too. Not just to keep out of the way of a mud flow. The island wasn't that big. If they could get to more than one ridge, they would surely see the remains of the housing in the settlement area. Buildings that would be sheltering the injured people they had come here in order to help.

'This way,' he said decisively, moments later. 'Follow me.'

The going was rough.

Steep and densely forested, trying to navigate across this craggy, subtropical island was a daunting mission. It might only be twenty or so square kilometres in area, Becca thought, but if you added the distances from rock-strewn gullies to surprisingly high ridges it was probably ten times as big.

Her legs were nowhere near as long as Jet's and the steps he seemed to take with ease were a difficult scramble for her, especially with the lumpy bag of supplies she had under her uninjured arm. And trying to suck in enough oxygen through a now sweat-soaked surgical mask.

It seemed crazy to be still wearing the masks. Totally incongruous that the sun was out, filtering down through the lush forest of palm trees they were currently climbing through. A breeze from the sea, now well behind them, was ruffling the palm fronds high above their heads but, unfortunately, it wasn't getting down to ground level. Becca was getting hotter and hotter, toiling behind Jet up the side of what felt like a sizeable mountain.

Her head ached, her arm hurt and she was extremely thirsty. How long had they been walking? An hour? Two, maybe. Jet was showing no sign of slackening his pace and Becca certainly wasn't going to be the first to suggest a break. She'd keep going, dammit. She'd show him that she could keep up. That she was as tough as she needed to be, like she'd claimed.

He wasn't talking to her and, for that, Becca was grateful. Not just because talking would have made it even harder to keep her oxygen level up. Did Jet share the weird feeling that they weren't alone on this journey?

That Matt's ghost was walking between them?

Oh…help… Becca needed to change the direction of her thoughts. Desperately.

'Hey…Jet?'

The response took several steps to come.

'Yep?' He didn't turn his head and he sounded vaguely surprised, as though he'd forgotten he wasn't alone. Was this the soldier in Jet? Totally focussed on the mission and nothing else? If so, it was a new side to this man. He'd always been very aware of those around him. Too aware, in some ways, able to pick up on things that people might have otherwise left unsaid. Becca didn't think he'd changed that much and that awareness was a more likely scenario. He was deliberately trying to blot out her presence because he would prefer her not to be here with him.

Well…tough.

'Do you think we really need to keep these masks on?'

Another short silence fell as Jet appeared to consider her query.

'The air looks fine.' Becca almost stumbled as she took her eyes off the ground to look up at the bright green canopy of palm fronds. The bright flash of a bird she didn't recognise flicked past and she could hear the calls of countless others around them. Patches of vivid blue could be seen and Becca couldn't help giving an incredulous huff of sound. 'It looks like such a gorgeous day.'

'Yeah…' Jet's tone was wry. 'We're lucky. The eruption's obviously over, for the moment at least, and we've got a good breeze behind us. Any volcanic ash is being blown towards the other side of the island. I'm hoping the settlement's on this side, as well.' He tugged at his mask. 'You're right. Let's ditch them. We've got more if we need them later.'

'Later' was like a piece of string. It could be any length at all. At least it felt slightly easier to breathe without the covering of fabric on her face.

'It's a shame the coast was too rough to get around.'

'Seemed like a good idea to get to higher ground and a bit farther away from the volcano.'

'How long do you reckon it'll take us to get to the others?'

'We're nearly at the top of this ridge. I'll tell you then.' He glanced over his shoulder. 'You OK to keep going for a bit?'

She wasn't, but something in his tone suggested he'd stop if she needed to, despite the urgency of his next goal. It made her want to ignore the aches that were getting bone deep and carry on. For his sake.

'I'm good' was all she said.

On they went. And up. Until, finally, the ground became less steep. The trees thinned and the landscape was changing. Becca recognised splashes of red amongst dark green grey foliage.

'Good grief. Pohutukawa trees. I feel almost at home.'

Jet didn't seem to be interested in the botanical features of this island. He did seem to be listening to something, however.

'Hear that?'

'What…the birds?'

'No…sounds like water.'

Suddenly Becca was thirstier than she'd ever been in her life. And hotter. A mirage-like image swam into her head. A mountain stream. A waterfall and a deep, still pool in front of it. She'd rip her clothes off and dive right in. Oh…she could almost feel the deliciously icy embrace of that water on her naked body.

And Jet would peel off his clothes and dive in right after her. He'd be submerged and she'd wonder where he was until she felt a tug on her ankle and squeaked in fright. He'd come up then, laughing…and then he'd pull her into his arms and…

Laughing? Jet?

What an absurd flight of fancy. A real smile

had always been at the top end of his happiest expressions. Laughing was far too joyous a sound to associate with Jet Munroe.

Had that always been part of the attraction? A recognition of an intensity that was part of her own soul? If so, they'd be the worst possible combination of personalities, wouldn't they? They'd probably fight like demons.

Or make love with a passion other people only dreamed of finding.

'Here.' Jet's voice broke into her wild fantasy ride like a bomb exploding. 'Let's stop.'

How had she not registered the increase in that sound? There *was* a waterfall. A fairly small one and there was no pool to dive into but at this moment it was almost a relief. The water bounced and splashed over rocks before disappearing downwards.

'Where's it coming from? Aren't we on the top of this ridge?'

'There's a higher ridge. See? It's like a stairway and we're on a bit of tread here.'

Peering through the trees, Becca realised she

could see more greenery instead of sky in the direction Jet was pointing. It wasn't a matter of a flattish hike and then heading upwards again, however. The disappearance of the stream revealed that a gully lay between this ridge and the next slope. How deep was it? Would they have to scramble right back to sea level and start climbing again?

It was enough of a setback to feel almost like defeat.

It could take them days to reach their goal. They might get there and find the other occupants of the island had already been rescued by ship. Would they think to send a search party for herself and Jet or assume they had gone down with the helicopter into the sea?

Becca sank down, still clutching her bag of supplies. Jet had put the life pack down. He eased the straps of the pack off his shoulders, arched his back to stretch it and then strode towards the stream.

The fact that he didn't even look tired made Becca feel even worse. The only muscles she had the strength to use right now were attached to her eyes and they didn't have to move much to watch what Jet was doing.

He scooped up handfuls of water and splashed them onto his face. He raked his fingers through his hair and used another handful to rub the back of his neck.

'That feels better,' he said in a satisfied tone. He turned his head, eyebrows raised in unmistakeable invitation. 'You should try it.'

'Mmm.' Her legs felt like putty as she tried to get up again.

Could she blame her weakness purely on exhaustion or did it have something to do with the image of Jet like that, with his hair in tousled spikes as though he'd just stepped out of a shower? With an invitation glimmering in his eyes…

He was in front of her now. Extending a hand to help her to her feet.

'I wouldn't drink it yet,' he said. 'I've got some sterilising tablets it might be prudent to use.'

The hand was irresistible despite the insistent

voice in Becca's head that told her ignore it and show him she was more than capable of leaping to her feet unaided. The grip was firm and warm and the upward tug made it so easy to stand up. Some of that heavy disappointment that they were still so far from their goal ebbed away. The touch of Jet's hand was like being plugged into a current of strength. A power source.

The cold water felt wonderful, even when it trickled down her neck and into her flight suit. She splashed again and again as Jet filled a specially designed bag with water and added a tablet. He set it on a rock to process and Becca sat beside it to rest.

'I've never broached the survival kit in this pack before,' he told her. 'It's got a lot of useful-looking bits in it.'

She leaned forward to look. 'Like what?'

'These water-purification pills. A good multi-tool. A lighter for getting a fire going. And... let's see what's in here...' He unzipped another waterproof pouch.

'We won't need a fire.'

Jet made a noncommittal sound. 'We'll have to see how far we get by nightfall. Don't think we want to be climbing near cliffs in the dark.'

So he was also thinking it could take them a long time to reach the settlement. He wasn't at all defeated by the prospect, though. He was simply thinking in terms of coping with it. Dealing with whatever obstacles presented themselves.

Becca could do that, too.

'Don't suppose there's any chocolate in there?'

'Something even better. Muesli bars.' Jet held up a foil-wrapped bar. 'Might be a bit stale.'

'It'll be great. Thanks.' Becca took the bar but didn't open it. 'I need a drink first, I think. Right now I'm so dry I wouldn't have enough spit to swallow anything.'

Jet held the bag up to the light and examined the contents. 'Should be done. There's a valve at the bottom. Pull it out and suck on it. Like a drink bottle.'

It was the most delicious liquid Becca had ever tasted.

'Take it slowly,' Jet advised. 'Don't skull.'

With the intention of giving him a scathing glance to let him know she knew what she was doing, Becca let her gaze drift sideways as she kept drinking. She was startled to find him staring at her intently, his expression unreadable. Her thirst suddenly slaked, she lowered her arm and handed the bag over to him.

'I'll fill it up again before we head off,' Jet said, accepting the bag. 'There'll be more later.'

She found herself watching him drink just as intently as he'd watched her. The way the muscles in his throat rippled as he swallowed. The way his lips were closed around the valve that her own lips had been touching only moments ago.

She should be getting used to this odd, unsettling sensation deep in her gut but it was getting stronger. What had Jet been thinking as he'd watched *her* drink?

And why did she have to be remembering that kiss yet again?

He'd been astonished. She'd read that in the tension in his lips instantly. Had relived it too many times in the weeks that had followed. But she'd also relived the sure knowledge that the surprise hadn't been unpleasant. His lips had softened. Shaped themselves to hers and moved with what felt like the same kind of wonder she'd been feeling in every cell. The sheer magic that sparkled into existence and had been just about to explode when they'd both heard the sound of Matt's voice in the hallway.

Becca ducked her head as she felt the heat in her cheeks. She busied herself unwrapping the muesli bar.

'I hope you've got dinner tucked away in there,' she said lightly. 'Just in case we do end up stuck out here for the night.'

Spending a night with Jet. Who would have thought? Becca didn't dare look up to meet his gaze because she knew he was watching her.

'Does that worry you?' he asked, a long moment later.

Was he kidding?

'No,' she lied. 'Not really.'

The silence hung between them like an unexploded bomb. Becca searched swiftly for something that she could use to defuse it.

'I did a survival course as part of my pilot training,' she offered. 'I can build a pretty good snow cave.'

'Useful.'

'I can make a brush shelter, too.'

'How 'bout a tree hut?'

That earned a glare. She was being at least partially serious here. Did he have to try and make her feel like a child again? That teasing note in his voice. Talking about things like Snakes and Ladders...tree huts...

'In case you hadn't noticed,' she snapped, 'I'm all grown up now, Jet.'

He still had a hint of a smile playing with his mouth but his eyes darkened perceptibly and became very serious.

'Oh...I've noticed all right.'

It was just as well Becca had finished her muesli bar because her throat tightened to the point where it would have been impossible to swallow anything without choking. It was hard to breathe, even.

It took her back to that kiss again. To the tiniest moment when they'd peeled their lips from each other's. A graze of eye contact that had lasted less than a heartbeat but she'd known the attraction had been mutual.

He might have denied it and ignored her. It might have been apparently destroyed by what had happened later, but it had been there.

It was there again now.

She couldn't look away. This was far more than an acknowledgment that she was an adult. A woman.

He was letting her know that she was a desirable woman.

That *he* desired her.

It was a moment she'd once dreamed of but now it was here and there was no way she could go there. It was way too complicated. Too painful. It *wasn't* going to happen…

Forcing herself to look away from Jet finally, Becca stared over his shoulder. Eyes narrowed but focussing on nothing. Simply trying to breathe evenly. Trying to gather up what felt like fragments of herself and put them back into some semblance of order.

Jet's voice seemed to come with the breeze that was making her skin prickle.

'Yeah...he's here,' Jet murmured softly. 'He always is.'

CHAPTER FIVE

THE second time she stumbled, Jet was close enough to turn and catch her.

'You want to stop again?'

'No. Not yet.'

It had taken them at least two hours to go as far as they could along the top of that first ridge. Now they were heading down into a gully and Jet reckoned that when they reached the next ridge they should be able to see the other side of the island and pinpoint their destination.

'Ditch the bag. You'll be able to keep your balance better without it.'

Becca shook her head. She'd carried it this far. She wasn't about to give up now despite how badly her arm was aching. 'You'll need the supplies.'

'They've probably got all that stuff in the first-aid kit at the station.'

'If it's not buried under rubble or mud or something.'

Something like molten lava? Their journey was bringing them closer to the volcano with every hour that passed. The blue sky had been left behind and it was a dense grey above the tree canopy and mountaintops now. Cloud or ash? The air still felt clear enough that they hadn't put masks back on yet.

Jet merely grunted in response, turning and moving on again. He had the harder job by far, choosing the path they were taking and pushing through any undergrowth. He got to test the footing, as well, and more than once a rock or rotten branch had proved unstable. Becca was sure she'd seen him limping for a while after one such incident and he seemed slightly more cautious now.

'Watch your feet,' he instructed.

That was precisely what she did need to do. She had to keep her mind on the job instead of letting it endlessly circle back to that gobsmacking comment Jet had made so casually.

He's here. He always is.

So he *was* just as aware of Matt's ghost as she was. And not just because she was here. The matter-of-fact delivery of the statement had been spine-tingling. It had been more than ten years ago but Jet made it sound as if it was still as much a part of his everyday life as…breathing or something.

The really piercing effect of the words, however, had been the whisper of sadness behind them. For the first time, it occurred to Becca that maybe she hadn't been the one who'd been most affected by Matt's death. The assumption had seemed justified. He was her brother, for heaven's sake. He'd been the most important person in her life since she'd been old enough to realise that he'd cared more about her than her parents had.

But they'd both been sent to boarding school at the earliest possible age and holidays had seemed few and far between. By high school, Matt had been in Jet's company day and night for months at a time. Well before the end of their schooling, they had been spending holidays as well as term time together. They had been inseparable so for the past ten years of Matt's life Jet had spent far more time with Matt than she had. And they had chosen their friendship, not had it there automatically because of family ties.

It was—astonishingly—conceivable that Jet had loved Matt just as much as she had.

That he'd been just as devastated by losing him.

She'd never allowed him that, had she? It hadn't even occurred to her when she'd blamed him for Matt's death. When she'd told him she hated him and never wanted to see him again.

She'd been wrong.

Just those few words and the eddies of emotion well below their surface had told her that. So convincingly it was impossible to stop thinking about them. Or to stop tears welling occasionally that were more than enough to blur her vision and make her miss her footing.

No one else in the world would have that connection. Even Max and Rick, while welded into the unit the four of them had made, had been a step removed. It was she and Jet who had been the closest to Matt and this new insight told Becca that Jet would understand how much the tragedy had affected her life. Still affected it.

How much else did they share as a legacy? The addiction to an adrenaline rush, perhaps, because it felt so good to still be alive when it was over?

Or maybe, like her, Jet's heart was walled off from loving someone enough to make them a life partner because it was safer than risking having them ripped away from you.

Talking to Jet about such intimate things was not going to happen. Even if she was prepared to expose her own soul, she knew that he never would. Not to anyone, probably, and certainly not to her.

Maybe he found it just as painful to be in her company as she had in his because of the memories it picked open.

Had. She'd put that thought into the past tense. Had something changed that much because she felt guilty about how she'd treated Jet back then?

Oh…yes.

'I'm sorry.'

'What?'

Dear Lord, had she actually made that apology aloud? No wonder Jet was scowling back at her over his shoulder. She couldn't tell him what she was really apologising for. Not yet, when she still needed time to get her own head around this shift in perspective.

'I'm...not keeping up very well. Slowing you down.'

'You're doing great.'

'You could leave me somewhere, you know... and send a search party after the ship arrives.' Becca could hear her voice trailing off. The thought of being left alone and watching Jet walking out of her life again made her feel astonishingly desolate.

His huff of sound was reassuringly dismissive. 'Not going to happen, babe. Even if I have to carry you.'

The thought of being carried in his arms to safety was the flip side of the coin with desolation on it. Happiness. Bliss, even? Becca didn't want to try and analyse that reaction.

'We'd better get there before the ship arrives or they might leave without us.'

'Why would they do that?'

'They might think we crashed into the sea and drowned.'

'If the emergency locator beacon was functioning, they'd see that we reached the island coastline. Plus I sent a message.'

'Really? When? How?'

'You were unconscious. There was a light flickering on the radio panel before it got too swamped with seawater. I sent a mayday. I also relayed that we were going to head for the settlement.'

'Oh...that's great.' Becca half crouched to slide down a steep bank between trees. Jet had paused at the bottom and was holding out a hand in case she needed help. She didn't, but when she stood up straight again she was very close to him and she looked up.

'Well done, you, on trying the radio. That makes me feel much better.' Her lips curled into a smile. 'Thank you.'

'Hey...no worries.' He was smiling back at her. 'I was looking out for my own skin, as well, you know. I'm not here purely as your guardian angel.'

It felt like he was. He had pulled her from the wreckage. Tended to her wounds. Was prepared to carry her through the jungle and across mountains if she couldn't make it alone.

She owed him a lot more than simply an apology for assumptions and accusations made so long ago.

Her head bent, as though weighed down with the heaviness of obligation, Becca trudged in Jet's wake and did her utmost to keep up with him and not slow him down too much.

Something had changed.

Somewhere in the gruelling trek they had been on for so many hours, the atmosphere had changed between them. It had been a gradual thing, a bit like the way the forest species changed from the palm trees to the pohutukawas or the way the sky had clouded over and the air temperature had dropped. Imperceptible while it was happening but suddenly you could see the difference.

Jet had become aware of the change in the moment Becca had smiled and thanked him because that smile had reached right into her eyes and made them glow with a warmth he'd never thought he'd see in her face again.

He could feel that smile touch places inside him that he'd forgotten existed but there was a poignancy in the sensation that made it almost physically painful. The pain was welcome in a way. It spurred him on as he led the way down the gully. Pushing on and ignoring the edges of exhaustion and the real physical pain in his ankle that was getting steadily worse. Thinking about Becca and that smile was an excellent distraction.

A window back in time. To a place where life had been as good as it got. The future had promised everything and more because, for the first time in his life, Jet had felt secure in a family unit.

And Becca had been a big part of that unit. A

bright, feisty kid who was becoming an extraordinarily beautiful woman who thought he was the second most wonderful person on earth.

Man, he'd loved that. Right from the start, when he'd seen how lonely she was, there'd been a huge gap in her life that he'd fitted into perfectly. That very first holiday, when Matt had taken him home to the Harding estate, the parents had been absent the whole time. Off on some conference in Egypt, apparently, that had included a cruise down the Nile and had been too good an opportunity to pass up despite the fact that it had covered the entire school holiday period.

Becca and Matt had clearly been used to being under the care of paid staff like the housekeeper, cook and groundsmen. The vast house had an equally grand setting with stables where Becca's pony had been kept, both an indoor and outdoor swimming pool, a home theatre and full-sized pool table in the games room. There had been trail bikes for the boys to play on in the surrounding countryside that had sparked the passion for motorbikes that had been the catalyst that had brought the 'bad boys' together.

Paradise for a teenage boy, in fact, as well as a chance to sample all the good things in life that Jet had only envied from a distance until then but, even as a confused and probably sullen adolescent, Jet had sensed the real gift he was being given.

Friendship and family.

The sense of belonging.

Of being looked up to as someone who mattered. Someone that people really cared about.

It had never been a hardship, giving up hours that could have been spent on the bikes or perfecting a game of snooker to entertain that small girl. Being teased had been a whole new experience for Jet. Being manipulated in a very unsubtle manner because someone was so determined to spend time in his company had been a pleasure all in itself. He'd learned to tease Becca back as he'd followed Matt's lead. They would spin the process out until nudging the boundaries of causing an upset but they would always capitulate. And she had always known they would.

At school, the bond had been with the three other boys and Jet had always watched their backs. Prepared to fight anything or anyone that threatened what was important to them.

Away from school that bond had been between him, Matt and Becca.

Fierce loyalty and an utter contentment when they'd been together.

He wouldn't have called it love. Maybe he wouldn't now, even. It certainly wasn't the soppy, warm-fuzzy stuff that most people associated with the emotion. It was more like a life force. Like…sunlight and rain. You could survive without them but when they were there, things grew and blossomed and life was an oasis instead of a barren wasteland.

The downward slope of the gully was levelling out. Soon they would start climbing again and Jet's instincts told him they were getting much closer to their target. Whether they could reach it before dark was another matter. They'd need to stop soon and drink something. Put their masks back on, too, because he could feel a change in the air they were breathing. Soon. But not quite yet because he wasn't ready to concentrate on the present. He needed to gather up the random shreds of memory and reaction and file them safely away.

It wasn't as though he didn't still have a measure of that life force in his life. He got it from Max and Rick and now there were others contributing. Ellie and Sarah and the kids. Baby Mattie and Sarah's boy, Josh. Jet wouldn't have admitted it in a million years but the addition of those kids to his inner circle of people was magic. The same kind of window back in time that Becca's smile represented. But now that he'd seen it again, he realised they were just a pale imitation of the real thing.

And that was why it was causing this peculiar pain. Because you couldn't go back in time. You couldn't change something as fundamental as the destruction of hero status and being sacked from the position of being the most important person to someone. As he had been by being blamed for Matt's death.

Becca had spent more than ten years blaming him. Hating him.

Why on earth would he think that one smile might mean that had changed? It wasn't the memory that was painful at all, was it? It was hope that her opinion of him had changed and that he could find his way back to that feeling of family. Hope that he knew would get crushed if he gave it any credibility.

He didn't even stop when the level ground was being left behind and a new and even tougher climb presented itself. It wasn't that he was trying to punish Becca.

He was punishing himself. For hoping.

Daylight was beginning to fade but Becca barely noticed.

She was numb to everything but the need to keep putting one foot in front of the other and breathe often enough to keep the burning sensation in her chest to a minimum. Taking her sunglasses off would help but the air felt gritty now and her eyes stung. Jet had produced fresh masks for them both when they'd stopped to drink the last of the bag of treated water a while back.

For ever ago. Becca had long since given up trying to keep any track of time. Her brain was as numb as her body but she kept going because if she didn't, Jet would pick her up and carry her and he had to be already hurting as much as she was. He was definitely limping and she'd seen the way he'd frozen for a moment to shut his eyes and deal with pain when he'd taken too much weight on that foot climbing over a rock not so long ago.

She'd have to see if she could help by strapping it up or something when they finally stopped.

If they ever stopped. Surely they were close to the top of this ridge by now. They might see the settlement building then and it would be stupid to waste hours waiting for daylight if they were within visual range of the people who needed them. The need wasn't one-sided, either. She and Jet badly needed the closest thing to civilisation on this island. They needed water and food and rest.

A place they could be rescued from along with everyone else.

Staying upright and continuing to move was more than an extreme challenge now. Becca slipped on something loose. Or maybe her legs just gave way. She had to grab at a scrubby bush for a handhold but that was loose, too, and it came away in her hand.

The whole bank seemed to be shivering. Moving. Becca was on her hands and knees. She lost her grip on the bag of supplies and items were spilling out and bouncing away down the slope. Clean, white bandages in their plastic wrappings seemed to glow in the gathering dusk. A loud, roaring sound increased and Becca was sure it was inside her head. She was about to faint, having gone past the physical limits she could push herself to.

Being gripped by her upper arms and hauled to her feet was unbearable.

'No! Just leave me, Jet. *You* go.'

Jet made no verbal response that she could hear.

He was dragging Becca, having abandoned the life pack.

Incredibly, the roaring sound got even louder and the night became a living thing—moving and breathing around them. And then the light changed, flooded with an unearthly, red glow.

Something crashed into the trees nearby.

Jet's oath was spine-chilling. He was moving faster and Becca was struggling not to fall again.

'Jet...'

'Move, Becca. We've got to find shelter. That was a rock.'

Another crashing sound came. The crunch of rock on rock. A burst of sparks and the strong smell of scorching.

Much later, Becca would marvel how much difference a burst of adrenaline could make. Muscles she'd thought were useless suddenly came back to life. Her thinking snapped into coherency.

The volcano was erupting again. Hurling missiles into the sky that were landing around them.

Lethal weapons, some of which were probably the size of a small car.

Because they were close to the top of this ridge, any cover they might have had from dense forest was gone. Trees were sparse here and bare, rocky formations offered no kind of shelter.

Or did they?

'There.' Becca tugged on Jet's hand, only now realising that they were joined by a determined grip on each other. 'Under the rocks.'

This bank of rock had an overhang. Not enough to call itself a cave but more than enough to shelter two people from airborne missiles. Maybe.

They were there within seconds and only just in time to save themselves from a shower of small rocks landing within metres of them. Some seemed to explode on hitting the rocks well above them and the sound and light show from the sparks made it all seem like some grotesque fireworks display.

Or how you would imagine the end of the world to look.

Another earthquake shook the ground beneath

their feet with a vicious jolt and Becca cried out in fear. They were about to die. Both of them.

I'm sorry.

Jet gathered the terrified bundle that was Becca into his arms and his only conscious thought was the awareness of a deep shame.

Not that it was a shame his life was going to end like this, in the shadow of an exploding volcano. It wasn't a bad way to go for someone who'd lived on the edge for so long. He might have chosen it, in fact. A sudden death in the midst of a dangerous adventure. Mind you, if he'd chosen it, he would have timed it a bit better.

Like when he was in his nineties, maybe.

No. The shame came from a sense of failure that he wasn't able to protect Becca and keep her safe.

He was failing Matt.

He was failing Becca.

Most of all, he was failing himself.

He wrapped his arms tightly around her and turned so that it would be his back that got any impact first. He used one hand to cradle her head against his shoulder, letting her bury her face so she wouldn't see what was happening. He even curled over her protectively, resting his temple on the top of her head. Both their masks had been ripped off somehow in the past minute or two and when he turned ever so slightly, he could press his lips against her hair.

He told himself he was comforting her but he knew he needed the comfort himself just as badly. He didn't want to die, dammit. Life was too precious and he still had too much he needed to do. And learn. New things to discover that he might not even know existed yet.

Like this…this incredible sensation of holding Becca that was unlike anything he'd ever experienced with a woman in his arms. This was so astonishingly…tender. No wonder he'd never gone looking for it. The sensation seeped into every cell of his body and made him feel curiously…raw.

Vulnerable?

No. He might have an excuse for letting the

volcano do that to him but Jet Munroe didn't do vulnerable. He'd learned not to at a very early age. Probably when he'd been a grubby kid with scabby knees and strangers had been telling him that his mother was gone but that they'd find some nice people to look after him instead.

If he thought of the shape he was holding as simply a frightened woman and not Becca, he might be able to lose that unpleasant sensation that was almost fear. It was OK to be afraid of the natural disaster occurring in the physical world but, if he was going to really protect himself, he had to back away from whatever explosions were happening somewhere in his mind. Or was it his heart?

She was a woman. A virtual stranger now, thanks to the years apart they'd had. But part of her was still the girl he remembered. The bond was still there and that made it impossible to simply let go.

And then Becca's arms stole around his waist and she squeezed him back, pressing her body tightly against his. She twisted her head to look up at him and because he was so close, with his lips on her hair, he ended up with his mouth only centimetres from hers.

She was looking straight into his eyes and whatever rational thoughts he was trying desperately to cling to shattered and vanished.

This was *Becca*.

And she was beautiful.

And he wanted her. He *needed* her.

Kissing her wasn't any kind of conscious action. It was the result of proximity. Of senses stretched to breaking point by what could very well be the last minutes of life.

Most of all, by sheer inevitability.

This had always been meant to happen.

Reality faded the instant his lips touched hers.

The nightmare became a dream. The culmination of many, many dreams, in fact. All the longing, the desire, the *love* that had been buried for so long came rushing back with the same kind of force that was still sending fiery missiles to land far too close to this precarious shelter.

It was a dream but it was real, too. The scratch of Jet's unshaven face. The incredible softness of his lips. The way his hands cradled her head as though she was the most precious thing on earth.

They were both filthy. Battered and bruised and sweaty and so exhausted it felt like being drunk, but none of that mattered at all. This was about...*life*.

Not just surviving. It went deeper than that. It was beginnings instead of endings. Wiping out a barrier that should never have been there. One that had walled off what was probably the most important part of being alive.

There had only ever been one man for Rebecca Harding and she was holding him at last. Touching him. Able to offer herself without the slightest hesitation or doubt.

The kiss was hungry. As though they were both tasting something they had wanted but been denied for ever. As soon as the pressure eased even a fraction, the contact was snatched back and deepened. Becca clutched at Jet's head, torn between gasping for air and being unable to tear her mouth from his.

And it wasn't enough. She pressed her body against his, wanting…what? To slip inside his skin? To be *inside* him?

No. She wanted him to be inside *her*. As physically close as it was possible for two people to become. It had to happen. This wanting was so powerful, she would shatter if it didn't happen. Dragging her hands from his head, totally unaware of any pain in her arm or anywhere else in her body, Becca fumbled for the fastenings of his jacket. Pulling it open so that she could find and touch bare skin.

He caught both her hands and held them hard. Stopping her progress. Did he not want this? Shocked, Becca looked up only to find the heat in the dark eyes so close to hers was just as wild as the fire inside herself. He did want this. As much as she did. He was just checking. Seeking permission to kick away any traces of a barrier.

In answer, Becca reached up to touch his face, running her fingers softly over his lips. She closed her eyes and tilted her head back. Offering him her throat. Sending her desire though her fingertips.

His lips were on her neck in a heartbeat. His hands unzipping her flight suit and peeling it back. They slipped underneath the T-shirt she had on and pushed her bra up so they could cup her breasts, his thumbs soft against nipples that felt as hard as metal.

The cry that carried over the roar of sound around them was unrecognisable and yet Becca knew it had come from herself. She was lost in pleasure so sharp it hurt. Desperate for more. To give as well as receive.

A low growl of sound that blended with the roar of the volcano came from Jet as her hands found their way beneath his clothing and touched what they were seeking. Maybe the sounds and the heat came from beyond this shelter but it seemed unlikely and Becca didn't care.

She gave herself up to ecstasy and the world outside simply stopped turning.

* * *

One day, he might look back and joke about the most explosive sexual encounter he'd ever had but laughter had no place in the aftermath of the unleashed passion that had just occurred.

Mother Nature seemed to be in tune with them. When Jet realised that the edges of paradise were blurring and eased himself gently from inside Becca, the night was very dark. Any glow from burning lava was gone. The eruption seemed to be over.

The roar of sound was gone, too, and it was suddenly so quiet he could hear Becca swallow. He could hear the rasp of the material her suit was made of as she unwrapped her legs and arms from around his body and moved to straighten her clothing.

The sense of loss was surprisingly sharp. Jet moved, too, to lessen its impact. He followed her example and tidied his clothing. Not that he had to do much. How on earth had they managed to have sex like that when they had been virtually still fully clothed?

The silence seemed to grow. He should say

something. But what? He knew Becca was watching him but he avoided her gaze while he tried to think of something he could say. Anything. Unfortunately, the words pounding in his head right now were not any he could release.

He had just made love to his best mate's little sister.

What would Matt think?

Maybe Becca would know what to say. She was grown up. Tough. She could handle anything, couldn't she?

Apparently not this. She was fully dressed again, sitting with her knees drawn up and her arms wrapped around them.

'Do you think it's over?'

'The eruption?'

He wasn't quick enough to avoid direct eye contact this time. The message couldn't have been plainer. He was an idiot. Of course she was talking about the eruption.

They both knew that what had just happened between them wasn't over.

Not by a long shot.

CHAPTER SIX

MOVING on was the right thing to do.

Jet would have been compelled to do *something*, in any case, given that the alternative was to stay there in the silence. With Becca.

With the knowledge that he'd opened the most enormous can of worms and he had no idea what he wanted to do about that.

The warning in that look on her face had been redundant. They had so much unfinished business between them, it would probably never be over. They'd made no attempt to discuss any of the issues of the past and now they had complicated it all to the nth degree by...having sex.

Was that all it had been? A wild coupling in the face of unbearable stress? A safety valve that had gone off because of too much pressure?

He was too tired and too shaken to be able to

think about any of it. He could see the worms. Impossibly tangled threads. Memories of events and their associated emotions, some of which he'd never dared try to analyse. The sex had been like a giant, emotional can opener and now it was threatening to do his head in completely.

Jet knew how to deal with such an overwhelming threat. He switched it off. Simple. It could all go into the 'too hard' basket for now. There would be time enough to debrief at some later, more appropriate time. If Becca would even concede having a conversation that involved the past, of course. What had she said?

Keep your memories to yourself.

The past was a no-go area. Whether they had a future at all was still in the lap of the gods. So the present was it for the moment, and Jet could deal with that.

'I've got a torch in my pack. I'm going to get to the top of the ridge and have a look around. Stay here and I'll come back for you.'

But Becca shook her head. 'I'll come, too.'

Any appreciation of how tough she was had

been switched off, as well. Jet was in soldier mode. On a mission.

'Fine.'

Becca gave a terse nod. 'Can I use the torch for a minute? I'll go and see if I can retrieve some of that stuff I dropped when the eruption started.'

He went with her but they could only find the life pack and about half of what the bag had originally contained.

'We're wasting time,' Jet decided. 'It doesn't matter.'

There was a strong smell of sulphur in the air so they dampened masks with saline and put them on. Jet sacrificed a crêpe bandage and they wrapped a layer over the masks for extra protection. The sunglasses weren't going to be enough for their eyes but there wasn't much he could do about that.

'I'll keep some saline in my pocket. We can flush our eyes every so often. It might help.'

'Getting out of here would help,' Becca muttered. 'A lot.'

Once they were moving, it was easier to leave

what had just happened between them behind. When they reached the ridge and could see the flames of a campfire that had to have been built by people, it was all but forgotten. They had an achievable goal and it was the destination they had been struggling to get to for far too many hours already.

'We'll go slowly,' Jet said. 'We should be able to keep away from any lava if it's got this far.'

There were trickles of fire to be seen well above them, trailing down from the glow that was the centre of the volcano. The air was thick and Jet couldn't decide whether his pounding headache and the vague fogginess in his head were due to his injury, his exhaustion or toxic fumes.

'How are *you* feeling?' he asked Becca a few minutes later. 'Physically, I mean,' he added in a silence that felt awkward.

'I've been better.' Her voice was muffled by the covering of mask and bandage but, even so, the tone was wry. 'Don't worry about me, Jet. I'll cope.'

She would, too.

Whose game was it now? Jet wondered as he led her downhill for the last time. Whose rules would have to be followed? If he wanted to continue playing at all, that was. It was a moot point. For the foreseeable future, he had no choice.

They reached what remained of the conservation workers' settlement within a couple of hours.

The small group of people sitting around the fire watched their approach in stunned silence. Becca stared back. She tried to smile but realised it didn't matter that she couldn't because her face was hidden anyway. It was completely overwhelming. Seeing these people. Smelling hot food. Knowing that—maybe within hours—a ship would be arriving at this location to rescue them all.

Knowing that survival was a real possibility now. If she hadn't been so convinced that her world was coming to an end, would she have given in to that passionate desire for Jet? Would it have been unleashed at all?

The time since then had been surreal. She'd

been in a strange, trance-like state where she'd still been able to feel exactly what it had been like when Jet had touched her. She could still taste his kisses. Feel him inside her. Hear his breath and the thump of his heartbeat. She could stay in that incredible moment when she'd felt...*whole* for the first time in her life.

It had kept her going. It had made the difficulties of the downward climb seem insignificant. It had made her forget about the parts of her body that cried out for rest. To begin with, at least, she'd been happy not to break the trance by talking. She'd wanted to keep it untarnished by any cliché or regret. But then the lack of communication had started to bite and the longer it went on, the more it strengthened the notion that, as far as Jet was concerned, it seemed like it had never happened. Had it just been a way to pass the time until they could get moving again? What on earth was he thinking about what had happened? About her?

In those few seconds of standing there, staring at the group of people that represented their return to the real world, Becca was snapped well out of any remnants of that trance. The thought that she and Jet might have to talk about what they'd done was both terrifying and inevitable. How could they not talk about it? But how could they talk about it without talking about everything else from the past?

Maybe the opportunity had already gone, anyway. They weren't alone any more.

Becca tried to say something in greeting to these people but that failed as much as the smile had. Her throat was too tight. She'd be able to blame the quality of the air for that. Or sheer exhaustion. If tears escaped, she could use the same excuses.

Jet didn't seem to be anything like as affected as she was, which only added weight to the fear that none of it had meant that much to him.

'Sorry we're a bit late, folks.' He was easing the pack off his back to put it down beside the life pack. 'Had a bit of a hiccup with the landing.'

'Oh, my God...' A woman stood up and came towards them. 'We knew you were due to arrive when the eruption happened this morning. We were sure there'd been an accident and that… you wouldn't have survived.' She was peering at them more closely. Taking in the wound on Jet's forehead and Becca's bandaged arm. '*Are you OK?*'

'A drink of water would be very welcome,' Jet responded. 'And then fill me in on what's needed here.'

Becca saw other people starting to move. Someone was bringing them water bottles.

'You must be hungry,' someone else said. 'We've been cooking sausages on the fire. It's nothing flash but there's plenty of bread and tomato sauce.'

Jet lowered his bottle and wiped a trickle of water from his chin. 'Sounds awesome but save me some for later. I'm here for the patients.'

'Jack's the worst,' a young woman said, her voice hitching. 'He's…got a bad head injury. And Roger…his leg looks awful.'

'Jack's conscious,' the first woman put in. 'But

he's not making much sense and he just wants to sleep.'

'Where is he?'

'Over there.'

Becca was beginning to realise why it was only a small group close to the fire. A tent-type shelter was off to one side and she could see people lying on the ground with others crouched over them. More people were over by the shadowy outline of a half-collapsed wooden building and sounds of hammering could be heard.

Jet was also scanning the area. He frowned at the sound of the hammering. 'You had people trapped, yes?'

'We got three of them out with only minor injuries, thank goodness. Adam's still stuck. His leg's caught badly. A couple of the guys are trying to shore things up to make it stable enough to saw through the beam that he's caught under.'

Jet's frown deepened. 'Do they know what they're doing?'

'Bruce is a qualified urban search and rescue technician. He's in charge.'

Jet nodded, clearly satisfied with the credentials. What would he have done if he wasn't? Becca wondered. Taken on an extrication task as well as patient management? Quite likely.

'Is Adam conscious?'

'Yes. He's in a lot of pain. We've got some pretty heavy-duty painkiller tablets here but they don't seem to have helped much.'

'I'll be able to deal with that.' Jet had his pack dangling by one hand. 'Jack and Roger had better be first on the list, though.' He waved his free hand at the life pack. 'Can someone bring that, please?' He was already heading towards the tent.

Becca had had a good drink of water. She shook her head at the sausage wrapped in bread that someone was offering her. It could wait. Picking up the life pack and following Jet might have been a kind of apology for losing most of that bag of extra supplies. Or maybe she simply wanted to be the one who helped him.

There were three people lying under the canvas awning. The area was well lit by kerosene lamps and the patients had blankets both underneath and on top of them. They even had pillows. Only one appeared to be unconscious and that had to be Jack. He had a bloodstained bandage around his head and a woman was sitting beside him, holding his hand.

'I'm Erica,' she introduced herself. 'I'm a nurse.'

'Excellent.' Jet unzipped his pack and started opening pockets. 'You can get me up to speed, Erica. I'm Jet Munroe, by the way. ED doctor and army medic. And this is Becca.'

Becca could see the way Erica drew in a deep breath, smiled and then released the breath in an audible sigh of relief. She nodded at Becca but the respect on her face increased noticeably as her gaze returned to Jet. If anyone could help Jack and the others, he could.

She put down the life pack, feeling a little out of place. Jet was a doctor. He had a nurse to assist him. A young and rather attractive one at that. It had been many years since she had worked as either a nurse or an ambulance officer and her skills as a pilot were hardly going to be help-

ful here. There wasn't that much room in the
tent so maybe she should go back to the fire and
leave them to it. She could have something to eat
except, strangely, she didn't feel at all hungry.

Nobody seemed to notice her taking a step
back. And then another, until she found herself
in a corner, where she sank down to sit, wrapping her arms around her knees. Exhaustion, and
probably very low blood sugar, were making her
feel spaced out. Oddly detached. As though she
wasn't actually here at all. She was invisible.
Floating above the scene and simply taking it
in. She wasn't consciously watching or thinking
about any of it, she was just there. Absorbing
what she saw and how it made her feel.

Jet remembered to pull some gloves out from
his pack and put them on. She saw him pause
and look up as he pulled the second one in place.
Looking for her? Because wearing gloves was
a kind of personal joke now—a thread of new
connection that had contributed to the resurrec-
tion of a much older and much stronger one? Or
maybe he was just getting his head around where

he needed to start work. The glance was brief, anyway, and didn't take in the direction that included where she was sitting so quietly. If he had thought of her at all, he'd probably assumed she'd done the sensible thing and gone to find some food and rest.

Which was exactly what she should be doing but she wasn't connected enough to her own body at the moment to make it happen. She watched Jet become the professional medic he was as he turned his attention to the injured people who needed him. The man with the bandaged head. Another with an injured leg. An older man who looked grey but had no obvious injuries to be seen. Jet talked to them. He laid his hands on them to examine their injuries. He pulled out gear and supplies to begin treating them.

He stuck electrodes on the first patient's chest and Becca could hear him quizzing Erica.

'How long was he unconscious for to begin with?

'Does he have any other injuries you've noticed?'

He cut away the remains of clothing around another young man's broken leg. Erica drew up the drugs he requested for pain relief and they talked about needing to straighten the limb. That would have to wait until he'd assessed the final patient here, the older man.

Utterly focussed, he managed to move with speed but it was obvious how thorough he was being. Becca had no idea how much time was passing as she sat there unnoticed. Maybe she even dozed for a while and some of her thoughts and impressions were a dream. About a doctor who was also a soldier. A real-life hero.

If these people were in any danger, Jet was the man to save them. They had known that back at headquarters, of course, and that was why they'd gone to the lengths of having him rushed to the rescue base by private plane.

But if he was so damn brilliant, why hadn't he saved Matt's life? Had he had the same abilities and skills as a newly qualified doctor? He must have had some of them. Maybe he just hadn't bothered using them on his best friend. Her brother.

The old anger was still there, wasn't it? Simmering not far beneath the surface. It made her feel more awake again and in a way it was almost comforting. Easier to accept than the wildly confusing feelings that had been aroused when Jet had been making love to her.

So Becca found herself nursing that old anger. Watching Jet with her eyes narrowed now, feeling even more detached from what was happening around her.

The nurse, Erica, was helping him. They were taking the blood pressure of the older man. Jet was putting in an IV line and Erica was hanging up a bag of fluids. Becca could hear the way they were talking to each other. Like trusted colleagues.

'What's his blood pressure now?'

'Gone up a bit. One-oh-five on sixty. I think we could give him a bit of morphine. Could you draw it up for me, please?'

'Sure.'

Her eagerness to help was almost palpable. So was how impressed she was by the man she was working with. Becca saw the way she was watching Jet's face as he injected the drug, rather than the patient or even the procedure.

What woman wouldn't be impressed?

Attracted?

What would Erica say if Becca told her that she'd had the best sex of her life with Jet during that last volcanic eruption? She might not believe her. Becca wasn't sure she believed it herself right now. Maybe she'd fallen down that slope and been knocked out again and it had all been wishful thinking.

She really needed to let go of that nebulous hope that Jet might have felt the same way she did. That them being together was written in the stars or something stupid like that. Watching Erica had just reminded her that Jet had always had, and probably always would have, women lining up wanting him. What on earth made her think she might stand out from the crowd? For old times' sake? Hardly, given that the 'old times' were too painful for them to even talk about.

Her exhaustion hit her full force now. Along with a wave of nausea. She had to get out of here and find some food and water. And some rest. Her vision was blurry. Perhaps that was why she didn't see Jet moving in her direction until he was crouched in front of her. Touching her hands.

'What are you doing in here?'

'Watching.'

'Oh...' Jet was frowning. He didn't understand. Becca wasn't sure she understood herself. Part of her had simply wanted to be near him. Another part was busy fanning the sparks of the old anger. It was all so confusing and she was too tired to think about it any more.

Jet's nod seemed to agree with her. He was too tired to pursue the matter.

He rubbed a hand wearily over his face. 'We've got things reasonably under control for the moment,' he said. 'Erica can keep watch. I'm going to go and check on Adam but it's time we both got some food and rest before we fall over.'

He helped Becca to her feet and led her outside. He disappeared into the half-demolished building for some time and she sat and waited anxiously, unable to eat until she saw him emerge safely.

'How is he?'

'Still trapped, but they've figured out a way of getting him out without collapsing the timbers around him. I've given him some pain relief and have some fluids running and I've told them to come and get me before they shift any of the weight. With a crush injury, he'll need careful management when he gets free. It won't be for a while yet, though.' Jet hunkered down beside Becca and nodded at a woman who was bringing them food. 'I've got time to take a break.'

They sat near the warmth of the fire and ate cold sausages wrapped in bread. They drank water. Someone even made them a hot cup of tea but then they were left alone. The people that weren't occupied with looking after the injured or helping with Adam's extrication had given in to exhaustion and were trying to get some sleep.

It felt like Becca and Jet were alone. Sitting in

front of an open fire in the middle of nowhere and in the middle of the night. The driftwood flames flickered and hissed softly, sending out tendrils of comforting heat.

'Mmm,' Becca murmured. 'I love fires.'

Jet made a soft sound, half chuckle, half sigh. Poignant enough to make Becca turn her head to look at him directly. And then, of course, it was impossible to look away. Shadows played on his face, making the lines sharper and his eyes far too dark to read, but he was looking back at her and his lips had a shape that Becca knew all too well. An almost-smile. It sucked her in every time and brought her way too close. Into danger-ous territory.

'What?' Her voice came out in a whisper.

Jet shrugged. 'I know how much you like fires, that's all. I lit your first one, didn't I?'

Oh…he was so right. In more ways than he would ever know. She'd told him to keep his memories to himself but this was different some-how. The memory of a happy time didn't seem so painful. Like the warmth and light of the fire they were sitting beside, it was oddly comforting.

Not that she was going to encourage it but she couldn't help thinking about it so she turned her head and stared into the flames to disguise her thoughts.

She'd been, what…nine or ten? It hadn't been the first time Jet had come home with Matt for a holiday. The boys had decided to camp out in the hills on a far boundary of the property and Becca had demanded to be allowed to accompany them.

The pup tent had been put up for her. Matt and Jet were going to sleep rough under the stars, like real outback men. They'd made a cairn of rocks and she'd helped to gather deadwood from the bush and there they'd been—just the three of them. Miles from anywhere, on a night so dark the stars had come alive, blazing like diamonds on black velvet. So cold that Becca had been shivering and so *big* that she'd been scared enough to think that maybe she'd bitten off more than she wanted to chew after all and she should have stayed home in her own bed. But then she'd experienced the thrill of those first flames leaping into the night.

'Do you still wish you were a boy?' Jet asked softly.

Oh...God. She had said that, hadn't she? Shouted it, actually, as she'd danced around the fire with a long stick, ready to poke the embers back into life if it was needed.

'I wish I was a boy.'

'Why?'

'Coz then I could light my own fires whenever I wanted to.'

The boys had rolled around laughing. It had seemed an eternity until they'd sobered enough to be serious.

'You'll be able to light as many fires as you want when you grow up.'

'Why do I have to wait that long?'

'Because you have to know how to control them. How to put them out if you need to. And you have to know the right places to light them or you can get into really big trouble.'

Becca could even remember the rider Jet had added when Matt had finished his brotherly advice.

'Fire's dangerous. Doing dangerous things can be exciting but it can also be wrong.'

She had her hand pressed to her mouth now, as the past somehow morphed into the present.

There'd been a kind of fire between them up on the mountain. More exciting than any she'd ever known.

Dangerous? Oh…yes. Why? Because it put her back into the place where she wanted to trust Jet. To offer him her heart. And that would make herself utterly vulnerable.

Wrong?

No. How could it have been wrong when it had felt so…right?

But maybe Jet felt otherwise. Becca slanted him a direct look.

'No,' she said quietly. 'I'm glad I'm not a boy.'

His face was very still and he waited a heart-beat before responding. 'Me, too.'

They were still staring at each other. He was

telling her he didn't regret their lovemaking. Maybe even that he wanted more? The moment stretched and grew. A turning point. A suddenly terrifying one.

Becca's heart was pounding. She felt dizzy. The whole world was spinning. She had to look away from Jet. To try and catch something solid.

Hang on! The warning came from nowhere. A wordless fear. The same one she'd had in that moment on the beach when she'd thought Jet had been sucked into the sea along with the wreckage of the helicopter.

Don't fall. You'll crash and burn.

'I get to light my own fires anyway.' Her voice sounded odd. 'If I want to.'

Jet grunted. 'Of course you do. You're all grown up now.'

Becca was holding her breath. What would he say now? That they had a new connection that was all about being grown up? Being a man and a woman? That it was too powerful to ignore?

But Jet stretched and looked away from her.

His breath came out in a sigh. 'Me, I just get to help put out the fires other people can't control.'

The moment had passed. They were back on safer ground now. Away from the past. Away from talking about what had happened between them or any connection they might have with each other. So he didn't want to talk about it. Or maybe the real truth was that he didn't even feel it.

That was more likely, given the way he'd been able to dismiss it and carry on as though nothing important had happened. At least it made it easier to hang on. Becca wasn't about to make herself look like a fool along with putting her heart at such risk. A fool who'd never got past a teenage crush.

She snorted softly at her own stupidity but managed to make it relevant to the conversation. 'Don't give me that, Jet Munroe. You light your own fires by choosing to go there. You love living dangerously.'

'Pot calling the kettle black, isn't it? Flying choppers for a living isn't exactly a quiet life.'

'So we're both adrenaline junkies. Nothing wrong with that, is there?'

'Hell, no.' Jet was smiling. 'Nothing like nearly getting killed to make you feel really alive, is there?'

It was Becca's turn to sigh. 'I'm not sure how alive I feel right now.'

Being able to relax for the first time since this day had gone so terribly wrong was making Becca aware of every ache in her body. She held up her left arm, flexing her fingers and then making a fist.

Jet grasping her hand was unexpected. Becca tried to pull free but the movement hurt and she sucked in her breath.

'It's got worse, hasn't it?'

'No.'

'Squeeze my fingers.'

Becca complied. This was a medical evaluation, wasn't it? Except…she made the mistake of looking up as she returned Jet's grip and suddenly the skin-to-skin contact was anything but professional.

Oh…Lord…

The depth in his eyes was disturbing. Had she really thought he was unaffected by the emotional side of what was happening here? That making love to her had simply been a way of passing the time? She was seeing something that she just knew no one else would be allowed to see. The turmoil of a man who didn't know quite what to do. Someone who was teetering on an emotional precipice and was feeling very, very unsafe. Like he was about to fall.

She hung on to his hand. Held his gaze.

It's all right, she wanted to say. *You're safe. We're safe, as long as we stay together. We wouldn't fall. We'd…fly.*

She took a deep breath.

'Jet…'

'Oh, my God!' The shout came from somewhere on the other side of the fire. *'Mandy… Steve…'*

Figures were emerging from the darkness. Coming from a different direction from which she and Jet had reached the settlement.

Other people came running. Amongst the cries of joy and hugging going on, it became apparent that Mandy and Steve and two others had been the people who'd gone on a night tracking mission for the kiwi breeding programme. They'd been missing ever since the first earthquake and here they were, having achieved an almost impossible feat of climbing around the coastline to get back. They were bruised and scraped but otherwise uninjured.

Had Jet been aware that he'd still been holding Becca's hand as they watched and listened to the joyous reunion? He certainly noticed as a man Becca hadn't yet met approached them.

'Jet? We're ready to get Adam free now.'

He let go of her hand instantly. 'Let me get my gear. You haven't lifted the beam yet?'

'No.'

'I'll be there in a minute.'

The man nodded. He looked totally exhausted but then he noticed what was happening around him. 'Good grief... *Steve*?' He moved away to greet the newcomers.

Jet was moving away too and all Becca could do was watch him go. She was too tired to offer to help and he hadn't asked. The opportunity to say anything had been snatched away from her and now she was wondering whether he would have wanted to hear it anyway.

He'd been eager to leave and get on with possibly the last medical challenge this rescue might present.

Relieved, maybe, to get away from her before she said anything that might have pushed him over the precipice?

She was on the same emotional ledge. Terrified of falling. Unsure of what to grasp that might allow her to pull herself back to safety.

Maybe they were both kidding themselves if they thought they could return to the safe place they'd been for the past ten years.

They'd started falling the moment they'd touched each other.

CHAPTER SEVEN

WHAT had Becca been about to say to him?

That she forgave him?

That she had missed him?

That look in her eyes… He could almost imagine that she'd been about to say, *I love you.*

And, for that split second, they were the words he had been waiting his whole life to hear.

Reality had snapped in, though, hadn't it, when those new people had arrived? The moment had gone so fast he wasn't sure he'd even read it correctly.

Even if he had, what was he thinking? Hearing those words would be about as terrifying as the seconds before crash-landing that helicopter, and at least then he'd had some idea of what he needed to do to attempt to regain control.

He wouldn't have known what to say to any

of those possibilities, especially the last one. It would be like those awkward minutes after the sex. Knowing that something important had just happened. That something needed to be said. And feeling completely...lost.

Just as well he had the default mode that allowed him to simply move into the next moment and do what had to be done rather than what should be done.

He went to supervise Adam's release. He gave the young conservation worker additional pain relief and made sure fluids were running freely into his veins to help dilute any toxins that might be released when the weight was lifted from his lower leg. He attached the life pack leads and monitored what was happening to his heart, breathing and blood pressure.

And then he saw what he had to deal with and any thoughts of Becca and the past were easily put aside. The arterial bleed from a partially amputated foot had been controlled by the weight of the beam and it proved impossible to control once they got Adam out. Jet fought for a long time with direct pressure and then a tourniquet and even an attempt to find the artery and tie it off.

Adam lost a lot of blood. He lost consciousness. In the end, Jet had to put in a nerve block and complete the amputation. The young man would have lost his foot anyway. He was not going to let him lose his life, dammit. By the time he was confident he'd won the battle and Adam was in the tent with the others, sleeping peacefully rather than exhibiting a dangerous drop in his level of consciousness, the new day had well and truly broken.

It was now more than forty-eight hours since Jet had slept and he had to catch an hour or two or he'd be no use to anyone. Erica was exhausted, too, but sure she could stay on top of monitoring the condition of the injured people until Jet had had some rest. For the moment all the patients seemed stable, though the oldest amongst them, Jim, was a worry. He had an internal injury that probably involved his spleen.

Jet raked his fingers through his hair, which felt

thick with grime. Backup was desperately needed but it couldn't be too far away now, surely. It was a new day. Someone could spot the big navy vessel on the horizon any time. There would be medical personnel and supplies on board. A mini-theatre, even, in case they needed to do an emergency splenectomy on their oldest patient.

Someone found him a blanket and a pillow and advised going close enough to the fire to stay warm. Jet was drawn back there anyway, because that was the last place he had seen Becca.

She'd offered to come and help with Adam but she'd stumbled in her exhaustion just trying to stand up as he'd gone past with all the gear he'd needed. He'd ordered her, in no uncertain terms, to stay put and rest. He'd told her that Erica had already been briefed to assist him.

He hadn't stopped moving on his way to the half-demolished building but he'd seen the flash of something like defeat on her face.

Loss, almost.

He remembered that look now, as he saw her again. Still in the same place. She had also been provided with a blanket and pillow and she was curled up, sound asleep, with her head cradled on her arm.

Her face was unguarded. A dark tangle of lashes on a pale cheek. A mouth that almost smiled in repose. She looked astonishingly young. Defenceless.

Jet lay down beside her. He closed his eyes but moments later he opened them again. He propped himself up on one elbow and gazed at Becca again. The pull had been simply too powerful to resist.

He was quite close enough to reach out and touch her face. To run a gentle stroke from her forehead to her chin.

Becca's eyes fluttered open, full of confusion, and then they focussed and her lips parted. She turned her head on a sigh. Just enough that her chin and cheek pressed into the palm that was cupping her face.

A gesture of gratitude?

It felt more like an acknowledgment of a connection too deep to put into words.

Without thinking, Jet leaned closer. He kissed her, very softly, on her lips.

'Go back to sleep,' he whispered. 'It's going to be OK, I promise.'

It took several seconds to come awake properly. The first thing Becca was aware of was how incredibly hard the ground beneath her was. And then she noticed how much her body was aching and how thirsty she was.

As she opened her eyes to bright sunlight, she was reaching out with her arm at the same time. Jet had been there, hadn't he?

Right beside her.

He had kissed her with such tenderness that Becca had allowed sleep to claim her again, feeling completely safe.

Or had it been a dream?

Jet wasn't there beside her now.

Becca sat up with some difficulty. She'd never felt so stiff and sore in her life. Her eyes felt gritty and the sunlight hurt.

Sunlight?

Squinting, Becca looked around. The sea was very close and blue. Tiny whitecaps were visible on the swells and seagulls circled overhead. There was no beach here. The waves broke directly onto black rocks but she could see that a jetty had been built and a dinghy with an outboard motor was tied down on the end of the structure. Presumably, ships anchored some way off the island and small boats were used to transfer supplies or people.

Stretching her back and wriggling her feet to try and warm up her muscles, Becca turned her head from one side to the other. Lush, green forest blanketed the craggy slopes inland and there, at the highest point, she could see a plume of smoke from the volcano.

Quiescent now, but she would never forget the sound of its wrath. Or the fiery glow in the sky and fountains of sparks. The deadly missiles that had sent her in panic to share that meagre shelter with Jet.

And she would certainly never, ever forget what had happened in that shelter. Even now, Becca could feel a sensation of pure pleasure melting the pain of overused muscles and joints. An exquisite liquid that was generated deep in her belly and trickled deliciously into her limbs, making her heart rate pick up and her lungs stretch to take in more of the surprisingly fresh air.

'Hey…you're awake. Want a cup of coffee?'

'Sure.' Becca blinked at the young woman near the fire.

'I'm Mandy. I wasn't here when you arrived. We were out tracking kiwi and got cut off by some lava. Took for ever to try and scramble back round the coast. You guys came overland, I hear?'

'Mmm.' Becca was getting cautiously to her feet. 'What time is it, do you know?'

'My watch got wet. I think it's late morning. 'Bout eleven?'

'Good grief, I've been asleep for hours.'

'You needed it. You're probably feeling a lot worse than I am and I feel bad enough.' Mandy smiled. 'Here you go. Sugar?'

'Please.' Becca stirred two heaped spoons into the mug. She needed a good energy boost.

'Want something to eat? I can do a honey or peanut-butter sandwich.'

She should eat but Becca shook her head. The hot drink was enough for now and there was an urgency about drinking it.

'Maybe later,' she said. 'I need to...'

Find Jet. To catch his gaze and then she'd know if it had been a dream when he'd kissed her like that. As though...as though he *loved* her?

'To see what's happening,' she trailed off, handing the mug back. 'Thank you so much. That was the best coffee ever.'

'I'll come with you,' Mandy said. 'Hang on a tick and I'll just make a coffee for Jet. He'll need another one by now. Black, no sugar, right?'

She clearly knew more than Becca did about Jet's coffee habits and was only too keen to be doing something to help him. How did he get women on side so fast when he went around scowling so hard and looking unapproachable?

As if she didn't know. She'd been more than

prepared to push herself past any known physical limits to keep up with him. And she'd been the one to grab that heavy life pack he needed before anyone else got a chance to. You'd think that never smiling and being so focussed on your job you could come across as surly would make others wary but, with Jet, it just seemed to make them make more of an effort to get noticed.

How had he got on with Erica during Adam's rescue in the night? Becca found out soon enough as she went into the tent that now looked like a mini-hospital. Jet was there, on the far side, crouched beside a young, bearded man who had a heavily bandaged leg raised on pillows.

Erica came into the tent behind her, carrying bottled water. She paused and smiled at Becca.

'I hope you got some real sleep.'

Becca nodded, feeling a bit ashamed of herself, but Erica's nod was pleased. 'You needed it. You missed the excitement, though.' The nurse's gaze shifted. 'Your man's a bit of a hero all right.'

Her man.

In her dreams.

He had been, though, hadn't he? Just for a blink of time, up there on the side of a mountain.

There was no way she could prevent her own gaze shifting to Jet. Soaking in the picture he made. He was taking Adam's blood pressure with a hand holding the disc of a stethoscope in place on Adam's elbow and using his other hand to release the valve of the bulb. His face was intent as he watched the dial clipped to the cuff around his patient's upper arm.

And, yes…he was scowling.

Absurdly, it brought the sting of tears to Becca's eyes and curled the corners of her mouth into a smile at the same time.

She loved everything about him. Even the surliness.

She could make him smile. How many others could claim that distinction?

'We had an operating theatre going,' Erica was telling her. 'Adam's foot was such a mess, he was bleeding to death.'

'Really?' Becca was still watching the doctor with his patient. She saw Jet's satisfied nod and he was saying something to Adam, who gave him a smile in return and a thumbs-up sign. The blood pressure was obviously at an acceptable level. How had Jet managed to get a patient in danger of bleeding to death into such a stable condition given the relatively primitive surroundings and limited medical supplies?

'He had to amputate the foot,' Erica said quietly.

'Oh, no... That's awful.'

But Erica shook her head. 'He would have died otherwise and *that* would have been awful. Adam's the nicest guy you could ever meet and we're all over the moon that he's still with us. I think he's pretty happy about it, too, and he knows he owes his life to Jet.'

Jet's status around here had clearly reached new heights.

'How are the others?'

Erica's smile was back. 'Jack's got a headache that he says is worse than any hangover he's ever had, and that's saying something for Jack. Jet reckons he's got a severe concussion but there's nothing too dangerous going on. He'll need scans and stuff when he gets to hospital.'

Jet was beside Jack now, shining a small torch in his eyes and then holding a hand up in front of him.

'How many fingers?' Becca heard him ask.

'One. Trick question, right?'

'Keep your eyes on it for as long as you can.' Jet moved his finger up and down and then from side to side, watching closely to see how Jack was tracking it visually.

Erica still hadn't moved to take water to those who needed it. The two women stood side by side, watching Jet.

Everybody was, Becca realised, scanning the interior of this makeshift medical centre. There were several onlookers. Like Mandy and some others Becca had yet to meet. And why wouldn't they all be watching? Jet was their hero. He was using his astonishing stamina and praiseworthy skills to care for them all. To save the lives of the people they cared about.

He was brilliant and she felt proud of him. She

loved him, as much as it was possible to love anyone. So why did she have this gnawing sense of unease? A kind of tension pressing in on her and making her feel restless?

The answer came when her gaze returned to Jet to find he'd finished assessing Jack and was looking directly at her. How long had he been watching her soak in the results of all his hard work? The hero-worship he had earned from all these people?

He looked…uncomfortable. Embarrassed.

And then it hit her. That moment of eye contact had ignited a connection that went further back than what had happened on this island. It came with a wave of pain. He had saved the life of at least one complete stranger here.

Why hadn't he been able to do that for his best friend?

There was nothing for Becca to do in here. Plenty of people were available for the routine nursing and companionship these patients needed, and Jet and Erica were there for anything clinical. Becca went back outside and somebody

made her another cup of coffee and then presented her with a doorstop sandwich thickly
spread with both honey and peanut butter.

It was hard to swallow, however.

A heavy knot seemed to have lodged in her
stomach. A weight that told her she still hadn't
forgiven Jet.

Sure, she could understand that he'd been just
as devastated by Matt's death as she had been.
She could feel bad that she'd made him feel worse
with her accusations. Knowing that might have
changed how she felt about Jet was enough to
erase the hatred but, however much she wished it
wasn't, the core of that ill feeling was still there.

The idea that he could and *should* have done
more. That by doing even the tiniest bit more, he
could have prevented the tragedy.

Did she still believe that?

Yes. Somewhere, deep inside, that belief was
still alive. A spotlight had revealed it lurking in a
recess and that light had come from the evidence
all around her here. In Jet's abilities to beat the
odds. To negotiate inhospitable landscape. To

save someone's life when they were bleeding to death.

Was part of why he'd been so affected by Matt's death due to feeling guilty that he hadn't done that little bit more? Maybe the answer to that had been telegraphed in the discomfort she'd witnessed when he'd seen her taking in what he'd managed to do on Tokolamu.

The knot inside her was a kind of grief.

She loved Jet but if she was incapable of forgiving him completely there could never be any kind of future with him even if he felt the same way. And that kiss had suggested he might.

Forgiveness implied trust.

Trust made you vulnerable.

Was she, in fact, prepared to make herself vulnerable? She had worked hard for a very long time to protect herself from the pain you could risk by being vulnerable. To prevent herself ever falling over that precipice.

Maybe she should just leave well enough alone. She had always wanted to be with Jet and have him touch her intimately. Now she knew the reality of it and perhaps a perfect memory was the best outcome for both of them. Why ruin it by digging up things that could only push them apart and make them regret what had happened here?

The navy vessel was sighted early that afternoon and even after it had anchored safely away from the rocks surrounding the island, there was still enough daylight to embark on the treacherous task of evacuating everybody safely.

The injured went first because it needed a huge team to carry stretchers over the rocks and down to the jetty. Despite the willing team of volunteers, it was a slow process. Getting from the jetty into the inflatable craft was tricky and then they needed to be winched up a daunting height to get on board the ship at the other end of the short journey.

Jet made the trip with every one of the injured. First Adam and then Jim and then Jack. He handed them over to the ship's surgeon and made sure his patients were settled and stable before returning to the island. The others could be taken off in small groups but the sun was almost setting by the time the last group had a boat available.

Becca was in that last group. Jet and Steve, who was manning the outboard engine because he knew every rock to watch out for, were a tight team by now. Jet hung on to ropes on the jetty, trying to keep the boat reasonably stable in an increasing swell. With his free arm, he offered support to each person making the controlled jump from the edge of the wooden jetty into the boat.

He made sure he caught Becca's uninjured arm and he gripped it firmly. No way was he going to let her slip and go into the sea between the dinghy and the jetty. A wave rolled past as she stepped out and the boat tilted sharply. Jet let go of the rope, caught Becca in his arms and rolled onto the bottom of the dinghy, ensuring that he landed on his back to provide a cushion for her. A whoop of approval came from Steve and the others on board clapped and cheered.

'Score!' Someone shouted.

The relief of being rescued, combined with exhaustion and the aftermath of adrenaline release, was beginning to make them all feel somewhat euphoric. Even Becca was grinning as Jet helped her up and onto the shelf seat along the side of the boat where she could get a grip on a loop of rope. Another two people to get on board and then they were off, skimming over the top of the waves, leaving the island of Tokolamu and its angry heart behind.

For the next hour or so happy chaos ensued as the rescued were assigned cabins and given access to hot showers and fresh clothes. Jet took advantage of all the facilities himself but only after checking again on all the patients. Jim was creating the most concern.

'BP's dropped,' the ship's surgeon told Jet. 'I've got some fresh, frozen plasma running but I'm not happy. We'll arrange a helicopter transfer as soon as we're within range but that's not going to be until morning.'

'Are you set up for surgery if it's needed?'

'Yes. Most we've ever done at sea is an emergency appendectomy, though.'

'Splenectomy's in the same ballpark.'

'You're experienced?'

'I've done a few.'

'Good.' The older doctor nodded with approval. 'Here, take this pager. I'll beep you if anything changes. Or would you like me to look at that cut on your head now?'

'It can wait. I'll clean up first.'

So Jet had a shower and put on some grey track pants and the white T-shirt he'd been provided with. He picked up the pager and clipped it to the waistband of the pants. Seeing the last glow of the sunset on the horizon through the porthole of his cabin as he got dressed, he made his way up on deck and to the stern of the now slowly moving ship. He wanted a final glimpse of the island that he knew would loom large in his memory for as long as he lived.

When he got to the railing at the stern, just over the churning wake, he found he wasn't alone.

Dressed identically, in the soft grey pants and a

white T-shirt that was way too large for her, was Becca.

With the backdrop of an island that was already looking small and a dying sunset that stretched as far as the eye could see across a vast ocean, Becca looked tiny. The urge to gather her into his arms and protect her was strong enough to immobilise Jet for a heartbeat as he joined her at the rail.

Protect her from what?

They were safe now. Heading away from the danger of this unexpected adventure and back towards their normal lives. So why this over-whelming feeling that there was something she still needed protection from? What was it?

A job she had chosen and clearly loved that was actually a lot less dangerous than what he chose to do with his own life at regular intervals?

The past? Would trying to sort out that tangle of unhappy memories somehow protect Becca from renewed pain in the future?

And why did that matter so much? Did he see himself as part of that future?

Yes.

No.

Confusion held him in utter silence. They stood there, side by side, staring at the shape of the island that was now being swallowed by the night.

Jet didn't do involvement with women. Not long term. He couldn't invite Becca into his life and then walk away from her, though, could he?

If he took that step, it would be for life.

And it would irrevocably change *his* life.

Could he even give her what she'd want? Or need? What she deserved?

Highly unlikely, given that he'd never been able to give it to any other woman in his life. He had long since accepted that he was a lone wolf. He had his pack, with Max and Rick, but he needed too much freedom.

He'd end up hurting her.

She'd end up hating him. The way she had for the past decade. Nothing fundamental had really changed, had it? How could it when they hadn't even talked about any of it?

With no conscious awareness, Jet had somehow moved closer to Becca. Their hands were touching where they rested, side by side, on the railing. He became aware of it because it was like an electric current. Stealing up his arm and into every cell of his body. When Jet looked up from his hand in a kind of wonder at the speed of that current, he found Becca looking up at him.

The night was closing around them. The tropical breeze caressing them was making Becca's newly washed, short hair do its utmost to curl. Her eyes were shining with an emotion he couldn't identify. Relief, perhaps, that they were leaving the trauma of the island experience behind?

Her lips were parted and he saw the tip of her tongue emerge to dampen them. Perhaps she was planning to be the first to say something but Jet didn't give her the chance. Maybe he didn't want to hear anything that might break the spell that had been suddenly cast.

So he bent his head swiftly and kissed her.

It was only intended to be a gentle gesture. An acknowledgment of something that was far more profound than mere sexual attraction. But how on earth could he have forgotten that explosion of heat that came from touching Becca like this?

It melted self-control, that heat. It spread like the volcanic eruption they had witnessed last night until it felt like his whole body was glowing with it. It radiated from his fingertips and yet he could feel even more heat coming from the skin they were touching. On Becca's face. On her neck. Under that T-shirt where they encountered the smoothest, most delicious curve of her belly and the tiny ridges of her ribs and then the soft swell of a perfect breast.

He heard her gasp as he cupped that breast, letting his thumb caress her nipple. He heard the tiny groan of surrender as she pressed herself into his hand and reached for *his* skin.

He also heard the insistent beeping that was coming from the device clipped to his track pants. The pager summoning him because someone was in trouble. Probably Jim.

Letting go of Becca was the hardest thing Jet had had to do in his life.

And that, in itself, was as strident a warning as the sound coming from the pager.

His voice felt raw. 'I have to go.'

Becca simply nodded. She stepped back and turned towards the railing again, gripping it with both hands. Jet heard the way she sucked in a new breath as he moved away and it sounded oddly like a sob.

And that was when he understood.

She did still need protection from something.

Him.

CHAPTER EIGHT

THE helicopter made a perfect landing on the designated expanse of deck at the stern of the ship.

'Nice.' Becca nodded.

With the loud whine of rotors about to slow to an idle, her admiring comment couldn't possibly have been overheard by the group of people standing around the stretcher but one of them looked up and mirrored her nod.

Maybe Jet was the only one of them who could appreciate the skill needed to bring a chopper down so neatly on a moving target.

It was what Becca had come on deck to watch so there was no reason to stay any longer.

Every reason not to, in fact.

Did she really want to watch the stretcher being loaded and the aircraft taking off again?

Jet was here with his patient. The man he'd

been with for most of the night, according to the ship's grapevine. Emergency surgery had been needed and then careful monitoring afterwards. Becca, like most of the others rescued from the island, had stayed up until they'd heard the news that the surgery had been successfully completed. With that crisis dealt with she had suddenly had as much sparkle as a deflated balloon and had gone off to the cabin she was sharing with Mandy to curl up in her bunk and escape into blessed unconsciousness.

Of course, it had been successful. Another life had been saved. She had expected nothing less. Just like she expected that Jet would climb into that military helicopter to accompany his patient to the nearest large land-based hospital.

Yes. He was about to exit her life with just as much drama as he'd stepped back into it. But did she really want to watch?

She might never see him again.

Becca swallowed hard. She tried to tell herself that it was a good thing. In the past two days, ever since the moment she'd set eyes on Jet again, her life had been tipped upside down and shaken violently. The physical trauma and danger were things she could easily deal with but the emotional roller-coaster was something else entirely. Nobody could survive this kind of turmoil unscathed and the problem was generated by Jet's presence. When he vanished, life as she knew it would at least have a chance of resuming.

It had to. Despite hours of sleep, gently rocking in that narrow bunk, Becca simply didn't have any reserve of energy or strength left. Not even enough to make her legs work and take her away from watching Jet leave so she stayed where she was and watched the stretcher being loaded and secured in the belly of the helicopter. Jet was talking to the army medics in their flight suits and helmets but then she saw him step back and the rear hatch of the chopper was closed and locked.

The rotors picked up speed and Jet was in a half-crouch as he got well out of the way. Becca saw the thumbs-up signal of the pilot and watched the skids lift smoothly from the deck. The chopper hovered for a moment, moved sideways and then banked as it gained height rapidly and left the ship behind. In no time at all it was a dot, disappearing into the horizon.

Still she didn't move. She watched the small crowd disperse. All the conservation workers who'd come to wish their colleague a speedy recovery and see him taken away filed through the narrow door to go back inside. The ship's surgeon and the crew members who'd been involved in the transfer went off to their work.

Everybody had gone. Except Jet. He came towards her and Becca's mouth felt dry. It was curiously hard to say something.

'How come you didn't go with them?'

'He's stable and he's in good hands. They'll be back later to transfer the others, anyway.'

'So you'll catch a ride then?'

Jet shrugged. 'Maybe I fancy an overnight cruise.'

Becca couldn't read his expression but he seemed to be watching her carefully. Gauging her reaction. Why? Was he choosing to stay with the ship because of her?

Because he wanted to be with her?

Oh…help. She had to look away and the vast expanse of the ocean was soothing after the focus she'd seen in Jet's eyes.

The deck was shifting under her feet far more than the roll of the sea could account for. She'd steeled herself to witness his departure. She'd been ready to deal with it and get on with her own life but the rules of this game were changing.

Or were they? This had something of the intensity of that moment by the fire the night before. If he was choosing to stay because of her, that meant he was acknowledging what hung between them. And, again, he was sidestepping. Changing the subject. Making a joke about being on a cruise ship.

Now it was her turn. If she said the wrong thing, did she get to slide down some kind of emotional snake? Instinctively, she knew this wasn't the time to get serious. She was being given a clear direction of what her move should be and that was to make some light comment along the same lines. About the failure of the last port of call to live up to the promise of the brochure perhaps? Or to wonder what the activities officer had in store for the passengers today? If she did that, would she find herself with a ladder to get to the next level of the game?

But, if this was a game, the stakes were too high. The implications of winning or losing would be with her for the rest of her life.

This was as huge as the volcano on Tokolamu.

And just as terrifying.

She hadn't expected him to stay.

But how could he have left like that, with the last image of Becca being her hands clutching the railing of the ship and her choked sob as she struggled for composure?

As hard as it would be, somehow they had to talk or they might be left with more than Matt's ghost haunting their lives.

He wasn't going to promise anything he

couldn't deliver but, at the very least, he had to let Becca know that he would never forget her. That she had a friend for life and if she was ever in any kind of trouble, he would move heaven and earth if he had to in order to help.

The prospect of parting on good terms had seemed entirely plausible in the early hours of this morning, when Jet had been sitting in the ship's infirmary amongst quietly beeping monitors and patients who were all sleeping peacefully.

Standing here now, close enough to touch Becca, Jet realised he might have been kidding himself. Maybe he'd just been dreaming up an excuse to stay a little longer because he couldn't face the notion of never seeing her again.

'It's just one night,' he said, aiming to keep it casual. 'We'll be pretty busy sorting out the other Medevac transfers for the rest of today but…hey, I've been invited to eat at the captain's table. Would have been rude to say no.'

He heard a tiny snort of amusement. They both

knew that high-ranking officials in military service would not appreciate being called a captain.

'Lucky you,' she said.

'The invitation apparently includes a partner.'

'Oh...'

He wished she'd stop staring out to sea like that
and would look at him so he might have some
idea of what she was thinking. She'd folded her
arms around herself as though she needed comfort.

He could provide that, if she'd let him. But she
wasn't the girl he remembered. She was grown
up and she could look after herself. She might
not want anything more from him. She might
have *wanted* him to disappear along with that
helicopter.

She didn't look so grown up right now, though.
Holding herself like that made her look tiny
and...alone. Even her voice was small when she
spoke.

'Got someone in mind?'

'Yeah...you.'

Her head swivelled and her gaze flew up to meet his and she looked…scared.

Jet groaned inwardly as he reached out and took her into his arms. Her body felt stiff but she wasn't trying to pull away. Jet held on, closing his eyes.

'I didn't want to leave just yet, Becca. Not before we've had a chance to talk. We might never have another opportunity and if that's the case, we might regret it. I know I would, anyway.'

It took more than a heartbeat but he felt the tension in her body ease. Then he could feel the movement of her head on his chest. A subtle movement but definitely up and down. Agreement.

He pulled back far enough to smile at her. 'So it's a date?'

'For dinner?'

'More like after dinner, I think. When we can get some time to ourselves. Somewhere private.'

'I'm…sharing a cabin.'

'I'm not.' Jet gave her an encouraging squeeze and then let go. 'I think I've been given an officer's suite. Lots of room.' It seemed important not to mention the bed. Or even think about it. 'It's got armchairs, even.'

'Lucky you.' A tentative smile shaped Becca's lips but it didn't quite meet her eyes. 'I'll see you at dinner, then. Can't promise I'll be dressed appropriately, though.'

'Can't see anything wrong with how you look right now,' Jet murmured.

But Becca was already halfway to the door leading off the deck. She didn't hear him.

It should have been relaxing.

A day on the high seas with nothing to do but rest and eat. There were books available and satellite television and even a movie put on for the extra passengers, but Becca couldn't concentrate on anything well enough to enjoy it.

Jet might have been absent physically, helping the ship's surgeon give everyone from the island a check-up between helicopter transfers of the others who needed hospital care, but he might as well have been right by her side as far as her awareness of him was concerned. Holding her hand perhaps, so that she could think of nothing more than the extraordinary feeling of how connected they were.

Kissing her, even, because she knew that she would never experience lovemaking like his from anyone else. Ever.

When it came time for dinner, Becca felt ridiculous being seated with the commanding officers of the ship in their immaculate uniforms, while she was wearing track pants and a T-shirt. Her apology was charmingly dismissed.

'Elegant clothing is a disguise that some people have no need of.'

The men waited until she sat down before taking their places at the table.

'Besides,' another added, 'we like to dress our guests the same. That way we won't mistake them for crew and put them to work.'

Becca smiled and nodded. And allowed her gaze to rest on Jet, who was seated opposite her and wearing an identical outfit. They were a matching pair.

And it was true. Becca could imagine him sitting there in a tuxedo, looking breathtakingly elegant and gorgeous, but it wouldn't change the way his body owned the space it was in. Or the way he held his head with that curious stillness that disguised how alert he was. It was pure Jet. So was that look in his eyes that told her they were more than a matching pair for clothing.

They were two sides of the same coin.

Desire warred with grief. They might never see each other again. She had to look away and try to focus on something else or she might do something incredibly embarrassing, like burst into tears.

It was a three-course dinner. The food and accompanying wine were delicious but Becca had no real appetite and she struggled to pretend she was enjoying her meal and not counting every second until she could be alone with Jet. With a supreme effort she did her best to seem just as engaged with the conversation going on around her.

By the time she excused herself and Jet followed her from the dining table, she was having difficulty remembering anything that had been discussed. Only two things had made enough of an impact to stay in her head. One was that the ship would reach dock at some point during the night so they would be able to disembark as soon as they woke. Transport had been arranged to take them to where they needed to go.

The other was that Jet needed to get back to his army base. He would probably be deployed on a new mission within forty-eight hours. Afghanistan was the most likely destination.

And, yes…he was looking forward to it.

So this was it.

An hour or two in his cabin to talk about things Becca had never wanted to talk about to anyone. And in the morning they would say goodbye and go their separate ways. Back to their own lives.

Jet could get killed in the next dangerous mission that would start within days, but even if he survived a dozen such missions it was unlikely they would ever spend time alone together again.

How could she say goodbye to this man?
How could she not?

By shipboard standards, Jet's cabin was luxurious. A wider than normal single bed, a small table and two comfortable chairs beside a smaller door that must lead to an en suite bathroom. The brass edging of the porthole gleamed in soft light that came from a bedside lamp. Maybe the same person who had turned on the lamp had also turned the bed covers back so invitingly.

It was still a small room. Just a few steps from the door to the chairs. An even smaller distance from the chairs to the bed. Jet's presence in this space with Becca seemed overpowering. Her legs refused to take her to a chair. Did she really want to be here?

Tilting her head, she found Jet looking down at her. There was a question in his eyes.

A plea?

She could see the same kind of turmoil she'd seen by the campfire two nights ago. The vulnerability that let her know that Jet had a patch of his soul that matched the one she worked so hard to hide. The lost and lonely part.

Yes. Of course she wanted to be here.

She wanted to reassure him. To let him know that, if he ever wanted to, it was safe to fall. As long as he was with her, because she'd keep him safe, no matter what it might take.

He wasn't saying anything and the tension in this small space lurched upwards. Becca could actually feel the pull Jet was exerting on her. She could feel herself tilting ever so slightly. Leaning towards him.

She could see the way Jet's Adam's apple moved up and caught as he seemed to swallow with some difficulty.

'So...' His voice was hoarse but he didn't try to clear his throat. 'You want to talk?'

'I want...'

You, her body screamed. Or was it her heart? Somehow, her head stopped the word emerging from her mouth.

Maybe it escaped through her eyes.

That might explain why Jet's pupils flared and swallowed his already dark-as-sin irises, making his eyes completely black. Why the atmosphere around them suddenly smouldered and crackled with suppressed fire. Was he trying to stop himself touching her?

Why?

This was only one night and they'd probably never see each other again.

The prospect was oddly similar to that belief they were both about to be killed by debris being expelled from an erupting volcano. Only this time they were safe. They had soft light and… and a bed.

They had all night. There would be plenty of time to talk. How could they possibly talk now when she, at least, felt like she was suffocating with her need to be touched? To touch in return.

Communication *could* be telepathic. Or maybe she'd made some kind of audible sound. Either way, the heat surrounding her was suddenly alive with tiny flames that licked at her skin. Jet gave a stifled groan and his head dipped until his lips covered hers.

* * *

What was he doing? He'd brought Becca back here with the intention of having an adult conversation. To tell her that he would always be there for her, for ever, but he couldn't give her what she might need or want in a life partner.

And she'd looked at him like *that*. As though he was the only thing she wanted.

Of course he could give her his body. For tonight, at least. It wasn't as if they'd be able to have any kind of conversation other than physical right now. Not when he couldn't string two coherent thoughts together, let alone words.

It might have been an adrenaline rush of danger and desire on the mountain but this was a whole different planet.

One that Jet had never been on.

Oh, he'd been with women often enough. He knew about soft lights and beckoning beds and how to take his time and wring the most out of every sensual second for both participants.

But it had never been like this.

Maybe the astonishing tenderness he felt came from having known Becca for years. The sheer wonder came from the miracle of how perfect a woman she'd grown into. And the mind-numbing excitement from an old whisper that this was illicit. It would be disapproved of.

Not by him, that was for sure.

And not by Becca, if her amazing responsiveness was anything to go by. The way her skin seemed to shiver when he touched it. Breathed on it, even. The way her nipples hardened instantly into tiny berries when he finally allowed himself the joy of putting his mouth to those small, perfectly formed breasts.

Her moist centre that would have told him she was more than ready for him even if she hadn't arched her body against his and cried out his name.

The sensation of totally losing his mind as he entered paradise at the same moment he entered Becca. The feeling that *this was it.*

He'd found it.

At last.

The tears came from nowhere.

Silently and softly, they trickled down Becca's

cheeks as she lay cradled in Jet's arms, slowly coming back to the real world.

The sex up there on the mountain had been astonishing. As good as she'd always known it would be with Jet, but *this*…this had taken her into a different dimension. Just as exciting but… different.

Heartbreaking.

The *tenderness* with which he'd touched her. The way he'd made her believe that she was special.

Loved.

That was where the tears were coming from. To truly love—and be loved—was a place Becca hadn't been in since her brother had been ripped away from her.

It was a place where life took on a whole new meaning. It *gave* life the meaning it should always have.

She didn't want to leave. Ever.

'You're crying.' Jet's thumb stroked moisture from her cheek.

'No, I'm not.' Becca pushed his hand away as she scrubbed at her face. 'I never cry.'

The careful silence told her that Jet was re-membering the last time he had seen her really crying. That equally silent, personal anguish she had suffered on hearing that there was no point in keeping Matt's life support going. The black, black time just before she'd turned her despair into anger and directed it at Jet.

That devastating time when she'd learned that you couldn't trust that loving place. That the only real meaning that life had was what you could squeeze out of individual moments.

This was one of those moments. She wasn't going to ruin it by thinking of the past. She propped herself up on one elbow so that she could reach Jet's face. She kissed him.

'I'm happy, OK? That was…' She couldn't think of a word to encompass the magic of what they'd just shared. She knew she'd never find it again. Damn…those tears were still far too close for comfort.

'Yeah…' Jet's arms tightened around her. 'It sure was.'

Becca found herself smiling. A wobbly smile, tinged with heartbreak but a smile nonetheless. 'Who would've thought?'

'Not me.' But then Jet sighed. 'That's not entirely true, actually. I *did* think. Once.'

'When?'

'At that party. Remember? When I kissed you in the kitchen.'

'I seem to remember it being the other way round. *I* kissed *you*.'

'Did you?' She could hear a smile in his voice. 'Guess it was so good I wanted to take all the credit.'

Becca snorted. 'So good that you proceeded to ignore me for the rest of the night so that I felt like a complete idiot.'

'I couldn't not ignore you. I had your brother giving me the evil eye. He'd already told me that I was exactly the kind of guy he intended to keep you well away from.'

'Oh…' That changed the memory significantly.

Jet had been attracted to her and he'd been hiding it? If only she'd known…

'And he was right. I'm not a good bet.'

'Oh?' Becca was still busy rearranging her memories of that night. Thinking of how different things could have been.

'I don't stay in one place for long. Or with one person. I'm a loner, I guess. Maybe you weren't so far off base calling me a gypsy.'

Becca was silent for a long minute. Aware of the warmth of Jet's body beside her. The rise and fall of his chest as he breathed. The steady thump of his heart against her ribs. Aware of how much she loved him. Of how different he was from anyone else she'd ever had in her life. He was a lot of things, this man, and all of them made him special. A gypsy. A pirate. A hero. A maverick. But a lone wolf?

No. His pack had been everything to him once. Maybe he didn't want to be loved but he *was* capable of loving.

'It's hard, isn't it?' she whispered into the silence. 'To trust someone enough to love them? Even harder to let them love you.'

She could feel the subtle tension gather in his body. He didn't want to talk about anything so personal. He was pulling away from her. Sadness crept back into the mix of emotions bathing her.

'Sometimes,' she added, almost inaudibly, 'it's lonely.'

That did it. Jet made a sound she couldn't interpret and rolled away from her. He sat up and then leaned over the bed to pick up his track pants.

'Want something to drink? There's a little fridge tucked in under the table.'

'No. I'm good.' Becca sat up but didn't reach for her clothes. She pulled the sheet up, bent her knees and wrapped her arms around them, watching as Jet fished out a can of beer and popped the top.

Finally, he sent a glance in her direction. 'I'm not lonely,' he said quietly. 'I have my life exactly the way I want it. And I have friends. Good friends.'

'Max?' Becca wanted him to keep talking,

even though it was hard to delve into the past. 'And Rick?'

'Yeah.'

'Do they do what you do? Never stay in one place or with one person?'

Jet grunted. 'They used to. Things have changed.' He took a long pull at his can of beer.

'Are they still practising medicine?'

'Oh, yeah.'

'Specialists?'

'Yep. We all decided early on where we were heading. Max is an emergency specialist, like me. Rick went into neurosurgery.'

Becca blinked. There were so many specialities they could have gone into as young doctors but they'd all chosen the fields that had been of the most significance when Matt had become so ill. Was there a connection?

'And they've got families now.'

'Really?' If the rest of his pack had changed, maybe Jet would one day, too. The bubble of hope couldn't be dismissed.

'Yeah…' Jet seemed happy to be talking about

other people rather than himself. He sat down in one of the armchairs and stared at the can of beer in his hand. 'Rick's with Sarah. She's got a little boy who's really sick with leukaemia and it turned out that Josh was Rick's son so he became the donor for bone marrow. I talked to him earlier today. There's been a bit of a crisis but it looks like Josh is going to be OK.'

'That must be a huge relief.'

'More than that, I'd say. I got the impression Rick's got no intention of letting Sarah out of his life. Maybe I'll get to be the best man this time.'

'This time?'

'Rick was the best man when Max got married.'

'Who did Max marry?'

'Ellie.' Jet chuckled. 'She's about as feisty as you are. She turned up on his doorstep and had a baby.'

'What? On the doorstep?'

'Pretty much. We'd just been out for our anniversary bike ride and there she was, banging on the door. Rick and I took off because we had a shift to get to and there I am in ED and Max turns up with Ellie in labour and trying to bleed to death.'

'Was it Max's baby?'

'It is now. You should have seen him when the baby was born. It needed kangaroo care and he sat up there in PICU doing skin-to-skin stuff with this tiny kid. I reckon he fell in love with Mattie before Ellie was even in the picture.'

Something cold and nasty washed over Becca. The kind of shock you'd get if you were lying in the sun and someone threw a bucket of iced water over you.

'Who?'

'Ellie.' Jet's tone was guarded now. He was frowning at Becca, clearly puzzled by her vehemence.

She sat up straighter. 'No...what did you say the baby's name was?'

She saw the way Jet closed his eyes, shutting her out. She saw his chest heave even though she couldn't hear the resigned sigh.

'Mattie. Short for Matilda.'

Or short for Matthew.

'How could he do that?' Becca's head was spinning, her tone one of puzzlement. 'What made him think he had the right to name a baby after Matt?'

'It's a special name for all of us, Becca.' Jet sounded weary. 'You don't have the monopoly on missing him, you know.'

'I don't believe this. How *could* he?' Becca was moving now. Finding her track pants and the damn T-shirt. 'He had *no* right.' She had to get out of here. 'None of you do.'

Even as the words burst out in that horrified tone, Becca knew she was being unreasonable. They had every right. As much as she did. And they had the opportunity, which was something she would probably never have. And maybe that was what was causing this pain.

'We weren't to blame for Matt's death.' Jet was standing up, watching her nearly frantic movements as she dressed herself. 'We did everything we could. *Everything.* If I could have done anything else...if I could have made it me instead of Matt that it was happening to, I would have jumped at the chance.' He swore softly. 'But you're never going to accept that, are you?'

Becca's could hear the bitter tone of his voice but his words were sliding past with no real meaning. She was still reeling from what felt like a physical blow. There was a child in the world who had been named after her brother. A sense that the 'bad boys' had more of Matt in their lives than she did.

Good grief…could this jealousy rather than anger be in any way justified?

She couldn't think straight. There were too many thoughts crowding her head. So many feelings jostling inside that she couldn't begin to know what she really thought. Anger was the easiest to recognise. To hang on to.

She looked at Jet, standing there, scowling defensively, and she could think of nothing at all to say to him. How could she begin to explain how she felt to someone who would be prepared to defend his pack—and any decisions they'd made—to the death?

However much she had once wanted to, she

had never become part of that pack. And now it was too late. They'd all moved on, without her.

And they'd taken Matt with them.

She was going to cry but no way was she going to cry in front of Jet and say things that would make her seem pathetic and needy. She was still clinging to the anger anyway and if she opened her mouth she'd probably say something that would only make things worse.

So she turned away.

And left.

CHAPTER NINE

NOTHING was the same any more.

Even his beloved superbike wouldn't start on its first kick. Hardly surprising given that it had been under a tarp for weeks in the basement of the converted warehouse he shared with Rick, but nevertheless it was yet another unsettling factor to add to the many others he had suddenly accumulated in his life.

Jet put more force into his leg action and the powerful bike coughed and then growled into action. He revved it into a throaty roar but his smile was grim rather than satisfied.

This was all wrong.

Here he was, about to embark on the longest road trip he'd ever made, from one of the southernmost cities in the south island of New Zealand to the very tip of the north island and…he was doing it solo.

It would have been unthinkable even a year ago. He would have had no trouble persuading Max and Rick to come along for the ride back then if they'd been able to juggle their rosters. They would have gone from Dunedin to Picton in a day, chilled out with a few beers on the ferry crossing between the islands and then had a great night out in Wellington. Another day on the road and a night exploring old haunts in Auckland and then a final blast up as far as you go north. He would have stood beside his mates by the lighthouse at Cape Reinga and pointed out to sea in the direction of Tokolamu island.

'Bet you're sorry you missed all that action,' he would have said.

And a year ago, six months ago even, they would have been sorry.

But nothing was the same.

He shouldn't even be back here in Dunedin.

Having left the ship early enough to make sure he wouldn't have to face Becca, Jet had got himself back to the army base to find they had nothing for him.

Correction. They had something he wasn't at all sure he wanted. A full-time career, training elite army medics. A commitment to military life that would probably have seen him excluded from active deployment. The army wanted him but someone up high had decided it was going to be on their terms from now on, not his.

He didn't like that. He'd stood his ground. Ultimatums had been delivered. They'd given him a week's leave to think about it.

So he'd come back to the closest thing to home that he had but they'd had nothing for him here, either. Locum positions in the emergency department were all currently filled. Of course, if he wanted a permanent position as an emergency consultant, that might be a different story. There was just such a position being advertised but they wouldn't take on someone who wanted to disappear for months at a time at short notice. You couldn't staff a hospital like that. Applications weren't closing for the job for a week or two yet. He had time to think about it.

Had someone on the hospital board of trustees been having a conversation with some influential acquaintance in the armed forces perhaps?

Had they decided it was time for Jet Munroe to settle down?

Jet rammed his helmet into place and pulled on his leather gloves. He coasted down the driveway and glanced both ways to check for traffic.

He was the only person who would decide when, if ever, he was going to commit to one career, thanks very much.

The road was clear. Leaving a faint rubber mark on the driveway, Jet took off into the dawn.

Everything had changed.

Oh, her apartment was still the same. So was her job when she returned after being forced to take a few days off to recover from the Tokolamu mission. She was wearing the same uniform, eating the same kind of food and seeing the same people she had known for years.

But nothing felt quite right.

Everything seemed flat. Almost pointless, in fact.

'You're very quiet, Bec,' her boss, Richard, commented. 'You sure you're ready to be back at work?'

'I'm sure. And I'd go stir-crazy if I had to spend any more time staring at my apartment walls.'

Not that the relative blankness of her walls was the problem, exactly. It was more like their ability to act as a movie screen for what was in her head. What was really threatening to drive her crazy was her inability to stop thinking about Jet Munroe.

'Hmm.' Richard sounded unconvinced. 'A crash is not a small thing to get through, you know. We've got some good people available if you want to change your mind about some counselling.'

Becca's headshake was definite. 'Don't need it.' She summoned a grin. 'You really think you could keep me away when that shiny new helicopter's just been delivered?' Her grin faded but she kept her tone light. 'What doesn't kill you makes you stronger.'

'There is such a thing as post-traumatic stress.'

'I know.' Becca had no trouble looking serious now. 'And don't get me wrong. It *was* a big deal. But I can handle it. Physically, I'm fine. See?' She held up her arm and flapped her hand. 'It was only a good sprain and maybe a mild concussion. I'm good.'

Her boss raised an eyebrow. 'It wasn't the physical repercussions I was referring to.'

Becca shrugged. 'I'm tough. I've been through worse.'

Which was true. Picking up her life and forcing herself to carry on after Matt's death had felt like wading through a mental swamp of sadness, with sinkholes of real depression to avoid.

Richard accepted her statement with a thoughtful stare and then a nod. He turned back to his paperwork with a sigh. Becca pushed her hair back from where it was tickling her forehead. She needed a haircut. She also needed to move, to try and clear the strength-sapping lethargy that was stealing through her body.

If only a job would come through. She'd been here since 6:00 a.m. this morning and it was now early afternoon and there hadn't been a single callout. Not even a transfer from a rural hospital into the city. She'd played with the new chopper, admiring everything more than once. She'd even warmed it up and given it a bit of a hover to make sure she was happy with the way it responded.

She'd hung out with her paramedic crew as they'd checked and rechecked all the gear, putting up with their ribbing about the extremes she'd gone to in order to get them new toys.

In desperation, she'd come up here to the office to try and find a distraction. Enough motivation to make her feel...*normal* again.

She stood up from the armchair she'd flopped into on arrival and paced across the office.

No death had been involved in this latest chapter of her life so why did she have this sloweddown, caught-in-a-swamp sensation again?

Because it *was* a kind of death, wasn't it?

She was standing beside the window now. Looking down at the patch of tarmac outside headquarters.

Had she really believed that her feelings for Jet had been buried and long forgotten? Effectively destroyed by nurturing anger and blame?

Her mind was only too eager to pull up the image of Jet stepping from that vehicle that night and it didn't seem to matter how often that scene was replayed. She could still feel an echo of the shockwave that recognition had generated.

And she only had to sit in the cockpit of a helicopter, as she'd already done that morning, going through the pre-flight check routine to remember the way the old feelings had started to creep back thanks to Jet's reappearance in her life.

To know that, deep, deep down she had been glad to see him. To spend time with him.

To know that what had really caused that first, overwhelming shockwave was the recognition of far more than the identity of a person. She had been looking at the missing piece of the jigsaw puzzle that made up the picture of who *she* really was.

So it was a kind of death she was having to deal with now.

The end of the possibility of ever feeling truly whole.

And, in a way, it was worse than losing Matt because the finality wasn't there. Things could have been so different.

If Jet wasn't so afraid to let love into his life.

If he wasn't such an adrenaline junkie who chased danger to make him feel alive. To give his life meaning. Becca knew that's what it was because she'd done exactly the same thing herself, all those years ago.

That first helicopter ride, when her passion had been born, had been what had pulled her back into living her life properly. The final escape from the edges of that horrible swamp. The buzz of the danger. Or was it, in fact, the buzz of feeling safe again? Knowing that you were alive simply because you could have been dead?

Her brain tried to catch that notion and explore

it more. There was something in there. Something important, but she couldn't quite catch it. Like a fragment of a dream that evaporated when you woke up. Instead, her mind whirled on, fast-forwarding to give her something else to angst about. Another reason why things had gone so wrong in the end of that precious time she'd had with Jet.

If only she hadn't reacted the way she had to the idea of a baby being named after her brother.

It was still a shocking revelation but that initial reaction had been so wrong.

Giving a new baby Matt's name was a lovely tribute. Maybe the only one they'd ever been able to make. The 'bad boys' had come to Matt's funeral. They'd stood right at the back, flanking the exit, wearing their leathers, with their helmets dangling from their hands, but they hadn't come to the graveside.

And Becca knew why.

It had been her decision to exclude them. To keep them from their rightful positions as pall-bearers. Her anger had been so huge. She'd confronted her parents and shouted at them. Told them that Matt would still be alive if his so-called friends had done a better job of looking after him.

That, if they were chosen as pallbearers, she wouldn't be attending her brother's funeral. She wouldn't speak to her parents again for as long as they lived. They would lose both their children if that happened.

Oh…it was still shocking. More so, perhaps, because the truth of it all was so clear. She'd done so much harm to everybody involved.

Most of all to herself.

She had pushed the 'bad boys' out of her life and by doing so she had excluded herself from what was the most tangible link she could have kept to her brother.

A place where his memory was so strong and important it would always be alive. Joy could be found in memories like that. In giving a new life a name that was so special.

She could have been a part of it.

She wanted to be—with all her heart.

But there was nothing she could do about it.

Jet was probably back in a war zone by now, doing hero stuff and saving lives. And, if she was going to survive, she needed to hang on to what she had and just keep going.

Becca pushed that wayward lock of hair that was almost a curl back from her temple again. She *really* needed a haircut.

The sleek black machine, with the figure hunched down to cut wind resistance, ate up mile after mile of the highway.

Jet bypassed the large metropolitan area of Christchurch, stopped briefly to refuel with the impressive backdrop of the Southern Alps on one side and the sea on the other in Kaikoura, and then kept going until he reached Picton and wheeled the bike into place on the lower deck of the inter-island ferry.

It was late afternoon on what had been a gloriously sunny day. The scenery, as they moved through the Marlborough Sounds, was stunning. Countless green islands in deep blue water so calm and glassy, the only disruption coming from a school of playful dolphins that was racing the ferry on its journey.

A journey that felt far too slow. Jet couldn't sit still. He didn't like someone else being in control of how fast he was moving. He didn't like being on a ship again because it reminded him way too clearly of being with Becca. Seeing her standing against the rail at the stern of the navy ship.

He stalked the decks, scowling harder at the cries of ecstasy from tourists who had spotted the dolphins. The cold beer he had purchased from the bar inside wasn't relaxing him nearly as much as he'd anticipated. Maybe it was the sight of so many damned islands out there and the reminder of Tokolamu and…inevitably, of course…of Becca.

Why couldn't he shut her out of his mind?

God knew, he was trying hard enough.

He'd been angry enough to be glad to leave her behind on that ship. The way she'd reacted to hearing Mattie's name. If he'd needed any proof that she was never going to put the past behind her and forgive him for his part in it, that had been it.

He'd told the others about it last night, when he'd gone to visit Max and Ellie. Rick had even been persuaded to leave Sarah and Josh at the hospital for a couple of hours and go with him, but if Jet had been hoping for an evening anything like the 'bad boys' would have had in the past, he'd been disappointed.

Disturbed, in fact. Almost as disturbed as he'd been when he'd first seen Rick again.

'There's no way I'm going to get used to that,' he'd decreed. 'I can't believe you went and shaved off all your hair.'

Rick had just grinned. 'Hair grows,' he'd said. 'It's no big deal.'

Ellie had shaken her head vigorously. 'It's a *huge* deal.'

Jet's nod had been approving. At least someone agreed with him. But Ellie's eyes were suspiciously moist and her smile was one of utter admiration.

'He did it because of Josh,' she told Jet. 'His

hair's all gone from the chemo and he felt like a freak and so Rick shaved his off to make him feel better. He even offered to shave Harry.'

'Who the hell is Harry?'

Turned out Harry was the disreputable-looking dog currently living with Max and Ellie but due to move in with Sarah and Rick and Josh in the near future. When Rick had sold the warehouse and found a more suitable family home, that was.

Jet drained his bottle of lager and debated going back into the crowded bar to queue for another one. He changed his mind when he saw that the ship was nearly at the entrance to the sounds. There were whitecaps on the open sea ahead. Maybe Cook Strait was going to live up to its rough reputation and provide a bit of excitement. A stiff breeze and a decent swell would send most of the tourists inside and Jet could enjoy the distraction of a decent bit of sailing in peace.

He needed...*something* that might make him feel less at odds with his own life. Nothing was the same all right. His whole world was in chaos.

The only home base he had was going to be up for sale in the near future because Rick was moving on with his life and the perfect bachelor pad was no longer suitable. Jet could buy the warehouse himself, of course. It wasn't as if *he* was going to need a family-type home.

But if he did that, there would be no good reason not to end up committing to a full-time job in the ED in Dunedin.

He'd be trapped.

His mates had partners now.

He'd be alone.

They hadn't even understood what it had been like having to see Becca again.

'She's a helicopter pilot?' Max had said. 'Wow. Matt would be proud of her.'

She wasn't just a skilled pilot. She was tough and courageous and feisty. Good grief….he was proud of her himself.

'She still blames us, you know. *Me*, anyway.'

'Nah…' Rick had shaken his bald head in disagreement. 'I don't believe that. She knows we did everything we could. Did you tell her how much we still miss him? That we go on our anniversary ride every year to honour his memory?'

'I told her that there was a baby named after him and she hit the roof. Said none of us had the right to have done that.'

The silence had been uncomfortable. Ellie had cuddled her baby and Jet had intercepted the look she'd exchanged with Max. They weren't about to let Becca's opinion undermine something so special to them. No one and nothing could diminish the bond they had.

The love in that glance had been the last straw.

The glue of absolute loyalty to the exclusion of anyone else that had held the 'bad boys' together as a unit for so many years had come unstuck. Rick had been unable to resist the pull back to the bone-marrow unit in the hospital, where Sarah and Josh were, a short time later, and it was then that Jet knew that he and Sarah would be sharing a similar kind of look.

He couldn't shake the chill of feeling excluded. A tug back to a time when he'd been an outsider. When he'd first arrived at Greystones Grammar school. An angry teenage boy who'd had nothing he could count on in his life. To those days before the 'bad boys' had come into existence.

It was then he knew he had to get out of Dunedin. To leave with the breaking of a new day and see if enough speed and distance might let him ride out the turbulence he had unexpectedly plunged into.

The heavy swell in the strait was great. Jet decided to leave his next beer until he got to his hotel in Wellington. It could be more than one, then. Maybe enough to let him get to sleep and not have his dreams filled with the taste and touch of a small, feisty helicopter pilot.

Finally. A job.

Becca was out the door and onto the helipad almost by the time her pager had finished buzzing. She was halfway through her pre-flight checks by the time her paramedic crew came running to climb on board.

She hadn't even waited to get all the details of the mission. 'Where are we going?'

'Coromandel peninsula.' Tom, the senior medic, was in the passenger seat beside her. 'A lookout on a hill near Cathedral Cove.'

'Cool. One of my favourite places in the world.' Becca programmed the GPS with a few, deft movements.

Her glance sideways was brief. It was a good thing that Tom was wearing the bright, red flight suit of the rescue service. If he'd been sitting there dressed in black from head to toe, it might have been a lot harder to focus.

'What are we going to?'

'Status-one patient. Under CPR.' Ben, the second crew member, was in the back, buckling himself into the seat. 'Sudden collapse. Thirty-nine-year-old woman.'

'Good grief!' Becca had the rotors turning now, picking up speed nicely. She reached to flick a switch on the communication panel. 'Flight zero three three, bound for the east coast of the Coromandel peninsula. Request clearance for take-off.'

The control tower responded immediately. 'Zero three three, you have clearance. Vector two.'

'Roger.' Becca lifted the chopper and used the designated air corridor to clear airport space. This wasn't going to be a long job but it was a beautiful day for flying and they were, hopefully, off to save the life of a person who was far too young to be having a cardiac arrest.

That she would get to test this new machine over her favourite country was a bonus. She loved the forests and beaches of this peninsula and the jagged mountain range often provided a bit of fun with weather and wind conditions.

Things were looking up. This was exactly what she needed to be doing instead of sitting around thinking far too much about things she couldn't do anything to change.

'I like it,' she announced, with a grin, a minute or two later.

'What? Being back at work?'

'That, too, but I was talking about this baby. He handles like a dream.'

'She,' Tom corrected, rolling his eyes. 'There are some rules that can't be broken, Bec.'

'Just as well you've never played Snakes and Ladders with me,' Becca muttered.

'What?'

'Nothing.'

'And just while we're on the subject of rules, Ben and I have made a new one.'

'And that is?'

'No uncontrolled landings while we're on board. Particularly when seawater might be involved. We don't want to get wet, OK?'

'No worries, mate. Been there, done that. Once was enough.'

More than enough. Not that Becca was about to admit it to anyone but her heart had skipped a beat or two on take-off that couldn't be attributed to the excitement or satisfaction of finally being given an urgent job to do.

Yes. There was a new thread of tension to be found in her career now. An awareness of just what it was like when things went terribly wrong.

It wasn't a bad thing. It might make her a much

better pilot because she would be a little more cautious and make sure she was keeping everybody safe. She would certainly think at least twice before she ignored instructions from her boss or anyone else who might have a better handle on the level of danger she was in.

That crash might never have happened in the first place if she hadn't had Jet beside her. Encouraging her to court danger because he was on exactly the same wavelength as she was. Becca sucked in a breath as she remembered those dark eyes gleaming with approval at her decision to flout authority and keep going.

They were way too alike. Bad for each other.

So, along with her new caution, it wasn't a bad thing that they were so apart now.

So why did it feel so…*wrong*?

Becca swallowed hard. Dipped her head as she turned to find distraction. 'Look at that…'

They were over the craggy landscape of the Coromandel Ranges already. The radio message that came through was an update for the paramedics.

'Ambulance on scene. Patient in asystole. CPR has now been in progress for sixty-five minutes and may be about to be terminated. There's a doctor on scene, as well.'

'Roger that.' Tom's tone was terse. Sixty-five minutes of CPR was unsurvivable. Especially if a doctor was present. Anything that could have been done in the way of drug therapy and defibrillation and intubation would have already been attempted. Was the mission about to be called off?

There was a slight hesitation on the other end of the transmission, as though the comms officer wasn't sure the next information would be welcome.

'The doctor is the husband of the patient.'

'Roger that,' Tom repeated.

Becca saw the glance he exchanged with Ben. There was no reason for them to continue when there was nothing they would be able to do. But there was a doctor there. A husband of a young woman who wasn't going to make it. If nothing else, their presence would be a courtesy for someone in the same profession.

'What's your ETA?'

'Less than five minutes.'

That clinched it. They were not ordered to return to base.

The location appeared deserted as they hovered over it a few minutes later. They could see the ambulance but its back doors were closed and there were no people to be seen. There wasn't even another vehicle in this small car park that was positioned to enjoy one of the most spectacular views you would find anywhere on earth.

There was just enough room to bring the helicopter down beside the ambulance. Becca landed, pointing forward, aware of how little space there was between the machine and a fence that kept people from going too close to the sheer cliff in front of them. Far below was the extraordinary blue of the sea and the irregular, green lumps of many islands. Turning her head to the side, she got a glimpse of the beach that was only accessible by boat or a long trek. Cathedral Cove was really two beaches, joined by rock that had an amazing, arched hole that allowed access to the second beach.

No. Actually, that wasn't all she could see.

Beyond the fence, crouched right on the edge of the cliff, was the figure of a man.

Becca turned to alert Tom but he and Ben were already clear of the chopper, stooping as they ran, carrying gear towards the ambulance.

Who was he? And what on earth was he doing?

Becca had been planning to let the chopper idle, ready for a quick getaway because there was nothing her crew would be able to do other than confirm death and offer sympathy, but she couldn't just sit here and potentially watch someone jump off a cliff. She shut the engines down and unbuckled her seat belt.

Less than a minute later she was climbing— cautiously—over the fence. She stopped a few metres away from the hunched figure. Frozen to the spot, she realised that she'd probably done the wrong thing here. She should have gone to get Tom and Ben. Or radioed HQ and got advice from Richard. There were bound to be protocols for dealing with this kind of situation but they hadn't been covered in her pilot's training.

She was doing exactly what she thought she was over doing. Breaking rules. Doing what *she* wanted to do without stopping to think about how it might affect other people. What if this guy looked up and saw her and that was the final straw and he hurled himself over that cliff?

He *did* look up.

Becca had never seen such desolation on any-one's face.

No, that wasn't true. She *had* seen just such a look once. In the mirror.

'I know,' she heard herself say softly. Her eyes filled with tears. 'I know how you feel.'

The man stared back at her. A puzzled line creased between his eyes. 'How?'

'I've been there.'

'You haven't. No one has.'

Behind her, Becca was aware that the ambulance doors were open. That there was someone lying on a stretcher in there but nothing more was being done for the patient. The ambulance officers, along with Ben and Tom, were all standing, staring in horror. At her.

It wasn't hard to put two and two together. Any further attempt to resuscitate the female patient wasn't a goer. The man close to her had to be the doctor. Her husband. The attempt at resuscitation had been stopped, probably only moments before their arrival. Why?

The man seemed to follow her thoughts as she looked over her shoulder and back again.

'There was no point in really starting,' he said brokenly. 'I knew that. But I had to try, didn't I?'

'Of course you did.' Becca sank down to a crouch. Somehow, she knew it wouldn't be a good idea to try and get too close. Because she knew how tender that space was? How unbearable the intrusion of a stranger might be?

'I lost someone once,' she told him. She had to sniff hard and swipe at the moisture on her face. She didn't need to tell him that she'd thought her world had ended. He would know.

'It wasn't your fault, though, was it?'

Becca's breath caught and she held it. Carefully. As though breathing out would do something terrible.

'She told me that she had a headache. I could have done something. I'm a *doctor*, for God's sake…'

No-o-o. Becca couldn't let her breath go. Couldn't take another one.

'She wanted to come for a walk at lunch time. Thought it might get rid of her headache. We got here and she said it was worse…she gave this awful cry and then collapsed in my arms…'

He was crying now. Racking, painful sobs.

'I didn't even have my damn phone. I knew she was dead but I had to start CPR… Had to keep going until a car stopped and I could send them to call an ambulance… Had to wait until someone else could tell me…

'It had to have been a subarachnoid haemorrhage.' The doctor was talking so quietly he seemed to be talking to himself. 'If I'd known, I could have taken her to Auckland. Got a CT scan or an MRI. They could have operated...' His cry was heart-wrenching. 'I let her take aspirin...'

Which would have made the bleeding worse but it was highly unlikely it would have made the difference between survival and death. His poor wife would have had an aneurysm. A defect in a major blood vessel in her brain. It had begun to get worse for some reason and then it had burst.

Just like Matt's had.

Jet and the others had known he'd had a headache. They'd been doctors, too. Matt hadn't wanted to go for a walk, though, had he? He'd wanted to sleep it off.

Had Jet ever felt this bad? So destroyed that ending his life might have been an option?

'It wasn't your fault,' Becca said fiercely. 'Don't ever think that.'

'How can I not?' The man shook his head. 'It's what everyone else will think. What am I going to tell the children?'

Becca's jaw dropped. There were children involved?

The doctor saw her face. As impossible as it seemed, his face grew even paler.

'Oh, my God…the kids…' He edged himself back from the cliff face. 'I have to get to the school…'

'Of course you do.' It was Tom talking, from close behind Becca. He stepped past her to offer a hand to the man and help him back over the fence. He glanced at Becca and she saw approval in his face, as though he thought she'd done something to help avoid further tragedy here.

But she hadn't done anything.

Except to relive a particular part of her life. From someone else's point of view.

To see just how much damage she had really done.

And she'd done it to the one person she truly loved.

It was unbearable.

CHAPTER TEN

THE plan had turned to custard.

He was supposed to have stopped in Auckland for the night. There were colleagues from his early days at Auckland General who would have been glad enough to see him. An impromptu barbecue might well have been organised by one of them and a reunion party would have gained momentum.

And maybe that was why Jet hadn't stopped to find a motel and make some calls, even though he'd already been on the road for too many hours today and was bone weary.

He would have been welcomed, he knew that. He was a minor celebrity amongst the dozens of people from med school and the wide variety of departments he'd cycled through as a junior doctor.

His identity had never been unique, though, had it? He was known as one of the 'bad boys' and it was the group as a whole that people had been drawn to. Even if he'd been the star attraction at a party, everyone would have been remembering the 'bad boy' who wasn't there any more and probably carefully avoiding the subject. They would enquire about Max and Rick instead, eager to know what they were up to these days.

Had he ever had a real identity that was all his own? His early childhood was a fuzzy blur of memories he'd rather not explore. 'Jet' Munroe had been born, in a way, when he'd arrived at Greystones Grammar and found that connection with Matt that had led to the others. They were the ones that had come up with the nickname and James Munroe had ceased to exist in any meaningful way.

There was only one person who might really see him as an individual. Might even understand and accept him, warts and all.

Becca.

Jet slowed his bike as he reached unsealed roads

and gravel spat in warning when he slewed sideways. He was in a semi-rural area well north of Auckland city. The rich farmland had been sliced into small 'lifestyle' blocks and their proximity to New Zealand's largest city made them some of the priciest real estate in the country.

The old Harding estate wasn't far from here. The place that had given the underprivileged James Munroe a taste of what it was like to have extreme wealth.

That wasn't what had subconsciously drawn him back, though. It was the taste of family he'd also been given.

That bond with Matt.

And Becca.

Not that he had any intention of going near the property. He didn't want to see the outdoor pool complex and remember the time he'd noticed that Becca was becoming such a beautiful young woman.

He didn't want to scan the hills because he knew he'd be trying to spot the gully they'd camped out in that night. When Becca had danced around the flames of that bonfire, yearning for the kind of adventures she'd thought only boys were entitled to.

Yes. She would understand him all right.

The memories would be waiting for him even if the property was no longer owned by the Harding family. Or was it? Jet knew that Becca's parents had died a few years ago. It had hit the news when they'd been amongst the unfortunate tourists that had been killed by that tsunami in Thailand.

Had Becca kept her inheritance? Funny that he'd never thought to ask, or even offer sympathy for the loss of her remaining family. The loss they'd really needed to talk about had taken precedence and even that had been engulfed by the tension of their situation and the form of release they'd indulged in.

He had to stop. He needed a break or he'd be putting himself, and possibly others on the road, in danger. Not just from his physical weariness but from the sabotage of thinking processes that any thoughts of Becca were capable of. Especially any that involved what had happened between them physically.

The old stone church up ahead on this road was an entirely logical place to pull over. Totally deserted on a weekday and heavily somnolent on a late, sunny afternoon. Ancient trees offered enticing shade and the scent of old roses hung heavy on the air. When Jet parked his bike round the back of the church and pulled off his helmet, the only sounds were the buzzing of bees and the clear notes of native bellbirds.

His whole body felt stiff after so many hours hunched over his bike. Hanging his helmet over the handlebars, he set off to walk a little and stretch. It was only when he turned the corner and saw the heavy wooden door set into the stone arch beneath the steeple that he realised exactly where it was he'd chosen to stop.

Custard was far too soft a word for what had happened to his plans. This was more like some kind of implosion. How could he not have recognised this place? OK, it had been ten years since he'd been here and the visit had been brief and awful, but this had to be the only church within a huge radius of the Harding property.

At some level, he'd known, of course. He'd simply ignored it and allowed himself to be drawn in. He must have wanted this.

Why?

A form of protest, maybe? Claiming the right he'd been denied all those years ago?

None of them had been welcome at the funeral as far as Matt's immediate family was concerned and everybody else there had been embarrassed by their exclusion. They all knew that these three young doctors should have been amongst the pallbearers. To be allowed to be with one of their own at the very end. To honour and respect a friend who was as close as any brother could have been.

Neither had they been allowed to be with him when they'd turned off the life support and let Matt die. They'd been out on the road together. Three 'bad boys' exceeding a speed limit on a back road not a million miles from here. They reckoned Matt had been riding pillion with them that day—the exit his spirit would have wanted.

But the funeral? They'd come late and stood in a silent row beside the door, holding their helmets. Jet had been holding two. His own, and Matt's. They'd left before the graveside ceremony. Before Becca could publicly shame them for not having done what they should have done, and saved her brother.

He'd never come back.

There would be a memorial to Matt somewhere in this churchyard and he'd never even seen it.

That was why he was here.

Maybe he'd known all along when he'd taken off on this lonely journey that this was where he'd end up. His life was in chaos. He would pick up the pieces and move on but a whole chapter of it was closing and he had to accept that first. Total closure couldn't happen until he completed what he should have done a long, long time ago.

It wasn't hard to find the headstone in the small country graveyard. A simple memorial that had only the name Matthew Samuel Harding and two dates, the year of his birth and that of his death. Jet didn't have to do any kind of calculation to know the difference was only twenty six.

The last of the day's sun pressed down on him as he stood, staring down at the headstone. It made him far too hot in his leathers but he didn't want to leave just yet.

'I'm here, mate,' he muttered aloud, 'but it's flippin' hot, isn't it? I'm going to go and sit under that tree for a bit.'

The oak tree was well over a hundred years old and the branches so heavy with acorns they drooped almost to ground level. Jet sat down, propping his back against the gnarled trunk. He was here, and it felt right. He would stay and soak in the peace and somehow something would fall into place and he'd be able to move on.

A tension he hadn't realised had been such a huge knot inside him began to ease.

Jet closed his eyes and simply let it happen.

Going home wasn't an option.

No way could Becca be in her apartment by

herself the way she was feeling by the end of her shift. The tragedy of the young doctor's wife had been the only topic of conversation as she'd flown her crew back to base.

'Poor guy,' Tom had said, not for the first time. 'He's going to blame himself for the rest of his life.'

'As if there was anything he could have done, anyway. Man, they're scary things, aneurysms. Who's to know we don't have a time bomb like that ticking away in our own heads?'

'Some people survive, don't they?' What was she trying to do? Becca asked herself. Find some kind of exoneration for blaming Jet? A plausible reason to have never totally forgiven him?

'Depends on the size of the bleed,' Tom told her. 'If it's small enough and you're close enough to a first-class neurosurgical unit, you've got a reasonable chance. A big bleed, especially if the brain stem's affected, the best you could hope for is to get someone on life support for long enough to make organs available for donation.'

'She would have had to have been in hospital

already for that,' Ben observed. 'Respiratory and cardiac function got knocked out almost immediately, by the sound of it.'

'Poor guy.' It was Becca saying it now. 'I hope he'll be OK.'

She'd told him it wasn't his fault and she'd been a hundred per cent sincere.

She could have been saying it to Jet with just as much sincerity and maybe, in her heart, that was exactly what she *was* doing.

Would she ever be able to tell him that face to face? It wasn't a question of forgiving him at all because there was nothing to forgive.

No. That wasn't true.

There was plenty that needed forgiveness but not from her. She was the one who needed to *be* forgiven.

The misery that had been circling for days was drawing closer and threatening to pull her under but Becca knew just how to deal with that. As soon as she got home, she stripped off her red flight suit and donned a very different set of clothes. An old, soft T-shirt. Tight black leather pants. Heavy boots that were very like her workboots apart from the silver studs that decorated them. A leather jacket with well-padded elbows went on last and she zipped it up and then fastened the studs on the flap that covered the zipper.

She collected her helmet from the table near the door and went out to her garage.

Her latest motorbike was only a couple of months old. She'd waited for its delivery with bated breath since she'd seen the advertisement and knew she had to upgrade.

'Light enough for a woman,' it had read, *'with power made for a man.'*

She'd been riding bikes for years but this was, indeed, something special. The speed and adrenaline rush of a good blast would be even better than the turbulence she'd unsuccessfully wished for on the way back from the Coromandel peninsula that afternoon.

Becca didn't give any particular destination any head room. She simply got out of the city and went for it. Only logical, really, that she found she'd taken a route so embedded in her memory it was automatic. Not that there was any point going near her property. She'd had it land banked and leased out ever since inheriting the acreage. She wasn't sure she ever wanted to set foot on it again.

There was somewhere else out here she hadn't been in a while, though.

The only place she could still feel close to her brother and talk to him without feeling like a complete head case. She sure needed someone to talk to today and Matt would have understood. Sorting her thoughts into words and just imagining what he might have said would help.

It had helped on more than one occasion in the past.

It was the throaty roar of a Ducati engine that woke Jet from a deep slumber in the long grass under the oak tree.

Someone was stealing his bike, dammit!

Leaping to his feet, he raced past the gravestones and around the back of the church. He could just see the sleek lines of his beloved black bike heading out of the churchyard. It took off with a burst of speed that sprayed gravel and raised a cloud of dust.

He skidded to a halt then, utterly confused.

His bike was exactly where he'd left it.

But it had definitely been a similar engine he'd heard and the bike had been black.

Who else would be riding a classy sports bike like that out here? Who would have wanted to come into an isolated place like this on a sleepy afternoon?

The answer came as he recaptured the image of the departing bike. He could only just hear it way up the road now but even from this distance he could detect something about the sound that wasn't quite what he would have expected. Less…grunty. He'd thought it was his bike, but what if it just looked that big because the figure on it was small?

Who else would come here?

He didn't need three guesses. How many

women were gutsy enough to be riding a super-bike, come to that?

But where the hell was she going now? She'd taken off in the opposite direction from getting back to town.

Kicking his bike into life, Jet took off.

He had no idea where this gravel road was heading. Fortunately it had straight stretches so he could catch frequent glimpses of the dust cloud ahead but it was proving hard to catch up.

Riding this fast on an unsealed road was crazy. Jet could feel his face settle into lines that got progressively grimmer as each minute passed. Not only was the surface of this road unstable, they were getting into hilly country and there were tight bends. He felt his own back wheel slip and he started muttering oaths that matched his expression.

This kind of behaviour was so reckless it was downright stupid. He could use his bike like it was an extension of his own body but he was struggling to stay in control here. He would have slowed down. Turned around and gone home, in fact, if it had been anybody else in the world ahead of him. Instead, his fury mounted and his speed increased.

Until he was right behind her. And still she didn't see him, so intent was she on pushing herself and her bike to the absolute limit. A dramatic spurt of speed on a straight stretch that actually lifted the front wheel of her bike into the air like some trick rider at a bike show. A sideways skid that had him catching his breath in horror but somehow she threw her weight and righted the bike from its dangerous slant. A bend that was so tight he could see her boot making a furrow in the chips of stone. A bend that went on and on.

And right at the end of that bend she lost it. The bike tipped just that fraction farther and then shot sideways with sparks coming from its metal. It seemed to increase speed as it hit the side of the road and became airborne. The rider came off at that point and, as Jet came to a slewing halt on the road, he could see the small, leather-clad body curl itself into a ball as it hit the ground and roll away downhill until it got caught in clumps of dense tussock.

The bike hit an outcrop of rocks much farther downhill. The petrol tank must have been punctured because there was a flash of flames, an explosion and then a thick cloud of black smoke spiralling into the sky.

The body of the rider was absolutely still.

Jet reached it in about three strides and didn't even feel his boots hitting the ground. He wasn't breathing as he dropped to his knees and rolled the body gently towards him. He had never been this afraid.

Ever.

Becca's eyes were open. Staring at him with disbelief.

'Am I dead?'

'Not for lack of trying.' Jet made no effort to hide his fury. 'You *idiot*. What the hell did you think you were *doing*?'

Where had he come from?

And why was he so angry?

Had she bumped her head with that spill? Nothing hurt. So she'd been going a bit fast, so what? Winning the battle of control over an adversary like an unsealed road was the kind of rush that made life worth living. As if Jet didn't know that as well as she did.

Carefully, Becca sat up. She eased her helmet off and tilted her neck to one side and then the other. Nothing hurt so that was good. She took a deep breath. Her ribs felt OK, too.

Jet was still crouched right beside her. Waiting for an answer.

Glaring at her.

'You know perfectly well what I was doing. You've done it often enough yourself.'

'I do not.'

'How fast were you going on *your* bike, Jet? To catch up with me? I *know* this road—the camber of every twist. I've done it a hundred times.'

'Hey...I wasn't doing it for *fun*.'

'Neither was I, dammit.' Becca glared back at him.

The frown lines on Jet's forehead seemed to

move. To become puzzled instead of angry. Some of the tension left his body and he sank lower until he was sitting beside her with the tussock making a surprisingly comfortable cushion. He fiddled with the catch on his helmet to take it off. It was still hot, even though the sun was well into its descent now. They had an hour or two of dusk and then it would start getting dark. It was very, very quiet. Apart from the occasional bird call, there was obviously no one else for miles around.

It was Jet who broke the silence.

'Then…*why*, Becca?'

She couldn't look directly at him. She needed to try and find the words. She also needed to find the courage to utter them.

'*You* know,' she said finally. 'When you cheat death and you're safe again, you can feel alive. Really alive. Like you're making the most of every second and…and you *have* to do that be-cause…'

'Because you don't know how many seconds you might have,' Jet finished for her.

Becca nodded. Whatever rush her ride had given her was wearing off. Things *did* hurt. Her shoulder was aching and there was an odd pain in her chest that made it hard to take a deep breath.

'And it's the same when you challenge yourself at work,' Jet continued. 'The bigger and scarier the challenge the better, because you feel safe when it's over and you feel like you've done something worthwhile.' His voice was so soft it was virtually a whisper. 'Like *you* are worthwhile.'

Becca rolled her shoulder with caution. It still worked. 'Doesn't last, though, does it?' she asked sadly. 'The thrill. That safe feeling.'

'No.' Jet's breath escaped in a weary sigh. 'I guess that's why people like us go hunting for it all over again. Why we keep doing dangerous, *stupid* things.'

'Like crashing helicopters.'

'And bikes.'

They both looked farther downhill at the smouldering remains of her motorbike. Becca shivered.

'I could have killed myself,' she said quietly. 'You're right. I am an idiot.'

Jet put his arm around her. 'Yeah…don't do it again, OK?'

Becca said nothing. She snuggled closer to the warmth of Jet's body, loving the feeling of his arm holding her so securely.

It took her back to those precious minutes of lying in his arms, in his bed, on the ship. Feeling like there was nowhere else in the world she ever wanted to be. Nowhere that could feel that safe.

And, suddenly, she could see the truth and it was so simple.

The rush you got by putting your body in danger and surviving was purely a physical thing. If you were brave enough to put your heart and soul into danger, the rush of surviving would be a safety that would never have to fade. You'd never have to keep hunting because if you found it and looked after it, it would just get stronger and stronger.

But you couldn't do it on your own. For the first time in her adult life Becca had to admit she couldn't rely only on herself. She needed someone else. Jet.

'You know why we keep doing it?' she ventured. 'And why that thrill gets harder to find so you have to keep doing bigger and more dangerous stuff?'

'Because we get good at it.'

'No. It's because we know what we're really scared of. We're happy to risk our bodies but we're too afraid to risk our hearts.'

The deep rumble of his voice could be felt as easily as heard. 'I'm not afraid.'

The way his arm tightened around her gave Becca a rather different answer, however. One that gave her the courage she really needed.

'I love you, Jet,' she said.

He made another rumbling sound. A kind of growl that was totally incomprehensible but it made Becca's heart skip and then soar as it chased away the last of that fear.

'You love *me*,' she said softly. 'That's why you came after me, wasn't it? Why you're so mad at me.'

'I'm mad because you've ruined a perfectly good bike.'

Becca said nothing. She just smiled.

After a long, long silence Jet bent his head to look down at her. 'Of course I love you,' he growled. 'You're—'

A final flash of fear came. Surely he wasn't going to say she was Matt's little sister?

'You're...*you*.' Jet's voice sounded curiously thick. 'I think I always loved you. But...'

'But you think there's no way we can ever be together.'

The silence was alive now. Tense. Terribly important.

'You think that loving someone and letting them love you is stupid because it's so dangerous. And that if you don't, you can protect yourself from ever getting really hurt.'

His arm tightened even more around her. Enough to make her shoulder ache harder but there was no way Becca wanted him to loosen that possessive kind of grip. There was an edge of desperation in the hold that squeezed her heart to breaking point and made that odd pain more intense. She didn't have a chest injury. She just had a heart that needed healing.

She slipped her arms around this man she loved so much.

'Have you ever stopped to think how much we miss out on by thinking like that? That *that* is what's really stupid?'

'Maybe…' The admission was cautious. 'Once or twice…recently.'

'What if we got told, right now, that we both only had a day to live? How would you want to spend it?'

'In bed.' She could hear the smile in his voice. 'With you.'

'Mmm.' Becca tilted her face up and found her lips only an inch or two away from Jet's. 'Good answer.'

The kiss was perfect. Soft and slow. So tender it made her melt. It could easily have grown into something much more passionate but Becca pulled back. She needed to finish what she'd started. For both their sakes.

'What if it was a year, Jet?'

'I'd still want to spend it with you.'

Becca gave a soft chuckle. 'In bed?'

'Not *all* the time. We could do something else in the daytimes.'

'Like dodging landmines in Afghanistan?'

'No way. You're not going anywhere near anything that dangerous.'

'Maybe you could be a flying doctor and I could be your pilot.'

'Hmm.' Jet was actually giving this serious thought. 'If we only had a year, wouldn't you want to have a bit more of a challenge? Use your skills to do something a little bit dangerous but really worthwhile?'

'Like what?'

'Oh…join Médicins Sans Frontières, perhaps?'

'Not a bad idea.' Becca thought about it for a nano-second. 'No, it's a great idea. Let's do it.'

'OK.'

'But what then?'

'What do you mean? You said we only had a year to live.'

'What if we don't? It's far more likely that we'll be some of the lucky ones and have thirty or forty or fifty years left.'

She could actually hear Jet swallow. He was holding her with both arms now. As though he never wanted to let her go. As though he couldn't.

'I'd still want to spend them with you. I'd want a house for us to live in and…and kids. A little girl who looked just like you.'

'And a boy?'

She could lose herself in those dark eyes that were fixed on hers. She could read exactly what was going on behind them, too. A little boy might look like her, as well. Like Matt. And she could see something else. Something she'd never, ever seen before.

'You're…crying.'

'Am not. I haven't cried since I was about six years old.'

Becca stroked the moisture away from his cheeks as Jet squeezed his eyes shut.

'What happened to Matt…it wasn't your fault,'

she said softly. 'I know that now. Can you ever forgive me?'

Jet cleared his throat. 'Don't need to.'

'Yes, you do.'

'No.' His eyes were open again, locked on hers. 'I forgave you a long time ago, Becca. About the same time I finally forgave myself.' He touched her lips with his. 'I love you. I can't spend another day away from you because…if you're not right, it might be the only chance I get to feel like this.'

Becca caught her lip between her teeth. 'Alive?'

He was watching her mouth but his gaze lifted to catch hers again. '*Really* alive,' he murmured. 'Like I've just been born or something.'

He kissed her again and this time it spiralled into much more than tenderness. Becca found herself pushed into the tussock but it put pressure on her shoulder and she winced. Jet drew back instantly.

'You *have* hurt yourself, haven't you?'

'Just a bruise or two. Nothing a soak in a bath and a good sleep won't fix. Don't suppose you could give me a ride back to town?'

Jet helped her up to her feet. 'Not a problem.' His grin was wicked. 'You don't really think you're going to get a good sleep, though, do you?'

Becca grinned right back. 'Not a problem. I can sleep when I'm dead.' She felt his hand tighten around hers and she squeezed back. 'That's a very long way off,' she assured Jet. 'I know I'm right. We're going to be amongst the lucky ones. We'll have the rest of our lives. For ever.'

'We're already the luckiest people on earth. We've got each other.' He started leading her up the slope towards where his bike was on the road but then he paused and smiled down at her. 'For ever is a nice long time, isn't it?'

Becca nodded happily. She dropped the helmet she was carrying and put both her hands around Jet's neck.

'But don't you go thinking that's a good excuse not to make the most of every second.'

She didn't need to exert any pressure to bring his face down to hers.

'I won't,' he murmured, as his lips covered hers. 'And that's a promise. I love you.'

Becca wanted to say it back but her lips and breath had been captured. She had to say it with her kiss instead.

And that was not a problem.

EPILOGUE

THE three men stood in close proximity.

Tall. Dark. Silent.

Clad in uniform black leather, motorbike helmets dangled from one hand. They each held an icy, uncapped bottle of lager in the other hand.

Moving as one, they raised the bottles and touched them together, the dull clink of glass a sombre note.

Speaking as one, their voices were equally sombre.

'To Matt,' was all they said.

'Yes,' a much softer voice chimed in. 'To Matt.'

The smaller figure making a circle with the three men had to stretch to touch her bottle to the others. She also had a motorbike helmet dangling from her hand and was dressed in black leather from head to toe, albeit with a few more decorative studs.

'Eleven years,' Jet said solemnly.

'And you've always managed to be together to make this tribute ride? Every single year?'

'Every year,' Max nodded.

'It's sacred,' Rick added. 'Always will be.'

'Sure will.' Max was smiling now. 'This marks another anniversary now, too. A really happy one.'

'The day you met Ellie.' Jet nodded. 'And Mattie was born.'

'I wish I'd known,' Becca said wistfully. 'About the rides. I used to go and put flowers on Matt's grave on the anniversary and sit there and talk to him for a while. I'll bet he was laughing at me coz he knew I was missing out on the fun you guys were having.'

'He comes with us,' Max said. 'Rides pillion.'

The others nodded. Jet's glance at Becca was a warning. 'That's all you're going to be doing from now on,' he said quietly enough not to be overheard. 'If that.'

Becca looked mutinous but Jet's smile had a smug edge to it.

'Let's join the girls,' Max suggested. 'The *other* girls,' he amended hastily as he caught Becca's glare.

Sarah and Ellie were in the kitchen as the small group came inside Max's house from where they'd been out on the terrace. They both exchanged glances with their husbands, understanding their absence but welcoming them back from a space they hadn't wanted to intrude on.

The 'bad boy' space.

Only now it was the 'bad boy and girl' space.

One girl, anyway. *His* girl. He could feel his chest having to expand to accommodate that warm, buzzy sensation. Pride? No. It was more than that. Way more.

Jet draped his arm across Becca's shoulders, loving the way her hair had grown long enough to tickle his hand. Loving even more the way she pressed in closer. As if it was exactly where she wanted to be—as close as possible to him.

'How was the ride?' Sarah asked.

'Awesome.'

A small boy with soft black curls was at the far end of the country-style kitchen. He was bent over, his hands firmly grasped by a baby, who was trying very hard to walk but had no balance. A large, shaggy dog was plodding beside them, watching the progress intently. The boy's face was tilted up, however, his gaze fixed on Rick.

'I'll be able to go along with you one day, won't I, Dad?'

'Sure.'

'Over my dead body,' Sarah said mildly.

Rick grinned and winked at Josh. 'I'm working on it,' he told the boy. 'We've still got plenty of time to convince your mum.'

Josh sighed theatrically. 'Becca got to go this time,' he grumbled.

'Of course she did. Matt was her big brother.' Max dropped to his haunches and held his arms out. With a squeal of glee, the baby let go of Josh's hands and hurled herself forward in a tottering run that could only end in collapse. Fortunately, Max had judged the distance perfectly and he swept the tiny girl into his arms and stood up.

'Did Mummy see that, do you think, Mattie?'

'She did,' Ellie smiled. She planted a kiss on the back of her daughter's head. 'Clever girl.'

'I'll have one of those,' Max said. 'I'm clever, too.'

Rick snorted. 'Who told you that?'

'Hey... I got us all together for the anniversary, didn't I? You said I'd never persuade Jet and Becca to come back from the wilds of South America.'

'Actually,' Jet said apologetically, 'we had to come back anyway.'

'Oh?'

They had everyone's attention all of a sudden.

'But didn't you plan on spending a full year with MSF?'

'They have rules, apparently.'

'About what?'

'About where you're allowed to be if you're pregnant.'

The silence was absolute for all of two heartbeats and then it erupted into cries of congratulations and everybody trying to be heard at once. Harry, the dog, let out a volley of excited barking and baby Mattie clapped her hands and shrieked joyfully. Rick and Max thumped Jet on the back and then hugged Becca a lot more gently.

Sarah and Ellie were both smiling through happy tears.

'How far along are you?'

'Twelve weeks.'

Sarah and Rick looked at each other and they both laughed.

'What's so funny?' Jet demanded.

'Well, we were kind of waiting for the right moment to tell you lot but—'

'I'm twelve weeks along, too,' Sarah told Becca.

'They'll be like twins,' Ellie said happily. 'Except…where are you going to live?'

'Haven't thought that far yet,' Jet said. 'We might hang around for a bit, though. We thought maybe it's about time we got, you know…'

'Married?' The squeal from Ellie could easily rival one of Mattie's.

'Your garden's had a bit of practice as a venue,' Becca said to Max. 'We were wondering if—'

'Yes,' Max interrupted, grinning from ear to ear. 'Of course. When?'

'Soon.' Jet and Becca spoke at the same time.

'It'll be the third wedding here,' Ellie observed. 'You guys are extra lucky, did you know that?'

Jet looked down at the woman he loved with all his heart and soul. She was looking right back at him and it was exactly the same look of love that was making her eyes glow like stars.

'Yeah…' His smile got caught. On that lump in his throat, maybe. 'I knew that.'

'I think we all are.' Max had one arm around Ellie now, with Mattie still tucked under the other arm. Rick was moving towards Sarah.

Josh eyed all the adults in the room. 'You're all going to do gross stuff like kissing, aren't you?' He sighed, even more heavily than he had last time. 'Come on, Harry. We're outta here.'

* * * * *

Mills & Boon® Large Print
Medical

March

April

May

Mills & Boon® Large Print
Medical

June

July

August